A Whitewashed Crow

Zeph Stone

Gray Man Press

A WHITEWASHED CROW

Gray Man Press
www.GrayManPress.com

ISBN-13: 978-0-615-35977-9 (trade pbk.)
1. Navy SEALs - Fiction. 2. BUD/S - Fiction.

Printed in the United States of America.

This novel is dedicated to all those who have passed through any segment of the SEAL training pipeline, whether they be current or former SEALs, drops who have gone on to serve the nation in other venues of the United States Navy, or those unfortunate enough to be under the weight of the BUD/S curriculum at this very moment. I hope this novel does a satisfactory job of representing you.

Contents

"A Whitewashed Crow soon shows black again."
– Chinese Proverb

Prologue

The economically sized University of San Diego dorm room would have been crowded if it were empty. Its dimensions were no larger than those of a standard single bedroom, yet it had been outfitted with accommodations for three. Three identical twin beds were stacked over three identical desks placed beside three identical wooden wall lockers. The arrangements had been leased to three first-year students, each completely different from the next with the exception of a common and routine desire for Friday night parties in celebration of one more week completed.

On this particular Friday night, late in the summer semester, the freshman housing building of Maher Hall was bustling with activity, inside and out. Coming from all directions and fleeing towards none were USD students of all shapes, sizes, and years, as well as countless visitors, invitees and crashers alike, both of other nearby campuses and non-collegiate organizations. Among them were military men, the majority Sailors but with some Marines, most stationed at one of the nearby naval installations.

"Thanks for offering but I don't drink," said one of these men. He was noticeably older than the majority of the other guests at the party, but could have passed for a senior if that's how he'd identified himself. His hair was dirty blonde and clean cut, not short enough to have labeled him as being a member of any of the armed services, yet not long enough to be out of regulations. His body was well developed and well muscled, but not enough to be turning any heads, especially in the company of bigger, taller, Division One collegiate athletes like those present at the night's gathering. His comfortably-tanned skin displayed no tattoos, only the hint of a scar peeping out from a healthy hairline which would never show the slightest sign of recession. The man's face and neck were smooth-shaven, like the faces of many of the men around him. It would have been impossible to guess what his eyes looked like, hidden behind the opaque lenses of his Oakley sunglasses, which he had become accustomed to wearing even at night. His posture made it clear to those around him that he was comfortable and relaxed in this setting, though his face showed very little emotion.

"I never thought I'd meet a SEAL who didn't drink," said a man whose boyish face suggested he was in his teens, but whose arms and chest insisted otherwise. The lean masses bulging outward from a fitted polo shirt were too much for any but the blind to ignore. Stemming from the top of the shirt was a powerful neck, thick enough that it would have implied to onlookers what musculature lurked beneath even if the man had been dressed more modestly. His face, perfectly proportioned and unscathed would surely have been that of a movie star if there were any hair to go with it. The BIC'd head altered the young man's appearance from that of an Abercrombie model to that of a convicted white-supremist trying to pass for an Abercrombie model. To compensate for the shaved scalp, the man maintained a friendly half-smile on what could, when advantageous, be a deceitfully expressive face.

"What makes you think I'm a SEAL?" The first man's tone of voice suggested he was somewhat irritated, but it might have been an irritation directed towards any combination of other factors. The over crowding of the tiny room was spreading inevitably outward into the hallway and surrounding dorms, but not quickly enough to keep up with the influx of new arrivals. The unmistakable scent of marijuana still lingered from the last dorm party. The deep pounding of the bass vibrations produced by two different songs erupting from the two sound systems in this dorm and that across the way were enough to make the windows shake.

"You're wearing a Navy SEALs T-shirt." The shirt was jet black and hung loosely on the man's wirey frame. Across the entire chest was the golden Naval Special Warfare Insignia. The decal consisted of a stooping eagle clutching in its talons an anchor, a trident, and an old flintlock pistol. The decal was accompanied by no label. No label was needed.

"Plenty of guys wear Navy SEAL T-shirts, especially in this town."

"The only guys who would wear one with a pair of 922s are real SEALs. The trainees who get issued the same boots know better than to parade around town in anything displaying a Trident before they actually get pinned."

"That's better spotting than I would have expected from the average college kid."

"Even the average college kid about to sign a contract to go to BUD/S?"

"Especially the average college kid about to sign a
contract to go to BUD/S. What do you want from me?"

"I saw a picture of you and one of your friends in the
newspaper, taken last Tuesday at the American Cancer
Foundation half-marathon and didn't find your name, but
couldn't help read that you're an instructor."

"First of all, Jonathon Stokley is not a friend of mine,
not by a long shot. And second, I've got better things to
be doing than entertaining some wannabe SEAL punk
looking for the secret to getting through BUD/S. I'll
answer one question and then you're going to leave this
party, one way or another."

"Okay, I've got a question for you," riposted a not-so-
average college kid no longer making an attempt to appear innocent and cordial. "Did you ever forgive Stokley
for taking away any chance you'll ever have of becoming
a real SEAL?"

1

The presence of the BUD/S compound itself was not nearly as imposing or majestic as one might expect after having heard all the stories of what goes on inside its bounds. It was a castle with no walls other than the flimsy chain link fences surrounding it on three sides, no moat save for the Pacific Ocean which bordered the compound on the remaining west side. It consisted of two lecture hall-styled classrooms, an array of office buildings, a supply depot shared with the Special Warfare Combatant-craft Crewman training program headquartered across the highway, and two barracks about a quarter mile apart with a small Navy Exchange Surf-Mart convenience store in between.

The final building in the compound was the BUD/S medical clinic. On a given day, it saw as much or more use than all the others combined, despite the reluctance of trainees to reveal any health condition which might put them at risk for medical separation, unless of course, they sought medical separation as a loophole around the inescapable shame of having 'Dropped on Request' or

'DORed.'

Surrounded by the extravagance of the famous, historic tourist town in which BUD/S found its home, this undersized training command would have seemed out of place to a passerby lacking prior knowledge of its existence and purpose. However, passersby with that particular point of ignorance were becoming fewer and farther between due to the perpetually growing infamy of the place. Countless tales of the grueling, some justifiably say dangerously so, training evolutions, as well as allegations of abuse against students by instructors (all of whom are current or former SEALs) had escaped from within and become the basis for books, movies, documentaries, bar stories, and more.

Most of these had been spread by the thousands of hopeful candidates to have come and gone since the program's inception in 1962, arriving one day, having eagerly awaited their chance to serve the nation in a tier one fighting force for months or even years, only to leave a week later with broken spirits and often broken bodies.

Seaman Apprentice Drake, however, was not one of those candidates. Seaman Apprentice Drake had no intention of completing his training here, nor had he ever. In fact, Seaman Apprentice Drake was not the least bit interested in any of the SEAL Teams or the roles they supposedly played in ensuring the fate of, what was from the typical American perspective: the free world. Seaman Apprentice Sidney Drake had, after nearly two decades of constant and profound achievement, abandoned a full-ride athletic scholarship to Stanford University, as well as the opportunity to compete with the university's men's water polo team in the upcoming Beijing Olympic Games for one reason only, and it had nothing to do with patriotism or a sense of duty.

    "Up."
Eight...
"Up."
Nine...
"Up."

Drake awoke abruptly, sweating lightly, the unrelenting echo of Instructor Hodges' repetitious cadence still sounding through his head as he mouthed out the word 'ten.' Drake, as well as the other 216 Sailors of BUD/S class 269 who had been lucky enough to avoid injury thus far and either too tough or too stupid to DOR from what many would argue is the world's most physically demanding military training, often dreamt of the program's exhausting evolutions, unwillingly reliving the many unpleasantries of a place slightly less hospitable than a maximum-security prison.

He identified the ringing of his alarm clock as the cause of his awakening and sprang out of bed to subdue it before it had a chance to disturb Ensign Jones, the short, African-American Naval Academy graduate who at this moment occupied the rack above Drake's in their small, two-man dorm on the third deck of Combined Bachelor Housing Building 302. He winced and cursed inwardly at the stab of numbing pain that shot up through knees and hips stiffened from the immobility of four hours of sleep. Knees and hips were the only thing that woke up stiff on these mornings.

With the curtain closed and too opaque to allow entry to the dim light of the moon outside, it was still too dark to see anything in the room, but there wasn't much distance between Drake's bed and the door, nor were there any obstacles in between. Apart from the wobbly bunk-bed structure he and Jones shared, the only other pieces of furniture were a pair of midsized metal wall lockers, rusted over several times from prolonged exposure to the local sea-salt air, and a small, semi-warped wooden desk with a mismatching but equally-warped wooden chair.

Drake was always the first one up in the morning. He appreciated the opportunity to survey a given situation before any of the other parties involved. This morning, he was the first Sailor in the compound to smell the salty aroma of the Pacific mist wafting through the barracks, the first to hear the waves crashing rhythmically into the surf zone beyond 'the berm,' the fifteen foot tall sand barrier that ran parallel to the west wing of the CBH. They sounded louder than usual, meaning they must be larger than usual.

Drake slipped on his shower shoes and zipped up his brown, polypropylene top. Coupled with a matching set of leggings, they comprised the cozy, BUD/S issue under-suit that served as pajamas for countless trainees in the unheated dorm rooms of the CBH during the chilly months of January and February. Stenciled in black fabric marker across the right pectoral of the top, exactly two inches from the seam of the zipper, read the name 'DRAKE.' Above it were two other names: 'CRAIG' and 'STRONG,' both crossed through with a single line. "I don't think either of them made it all the way," one of Drake's instructors had told him during his pass through the Naval Special Warfare Preparatory Course at Great Lakes Naval Station in Illinois a few months prior, "but maybe the third time's a charm."

He crept silently across the room to the door on the wall opposite his rack. Before undoing the deadbolt and opening the door, he performed an active check of his water wallet to make sure the second inside pocket contained his room key. He stepped lightly into the hallway, flexing his feet tightly to keep his sandals from clapping on the hard tile floor, and eased the door shut and handle back into place with such methodical care even he couldn't hear it latching.

Drake wandered, wearily but alertly, down to the exterior door at the north end of, what seemed to chronically knotted calves, an impossibly long hallway, outside onto the exterior stairwell and into the brisk morning breeze. He began to make his way westward over the berm and down to the waterline of the beach which, during high tide, was no more than fifty yards from the entrance to the ground-level gear drying cages adjacent to the west wing of the CBH. They emitted a moldy, salty, sandy stench as Drake passed, a stench with which he had reluctantly become familiar. At least the stench didn't flow into his window, only a few yards above, during the night while he was trying to enjoy what little sleep he was permitted by a schedule requiring more hours than any day could provide.

As he made his way nonchalantly towards the beach, Drake walked through an array of several dozen pull-up bars of various heights, implanted in the sand for use by the SEAL trainees and instructors alike during their regular physical training, or 'PT' sessions. He hesitated for a moment, tempted to perform a few repetitions before moving on. 'No,' he thought, better to save his strength for the day's formal training evolutions, which were sure to be every bit as demanding as those he had been put through the day before, and the day before that, and the day before that. He would need enough energy to perform to the high standard set by his instructor staff, as well as maintain constant situational awareness until his class was scheduled to be secured from training for the day, and that would be at least sixteen hours from now.

As he approached the water's edge, Drake could see that the waves were, as he had suspected, significantly higher than any he had seen so far during his stay in Coronado. Those rolling in nearest to him appeared to be about seven feet tall, just short enough to allow him to detect the choppiness of the waters farther off shore in which he and over two hundred other SEAL candidates would be swimming this afternoon.

The water before Drake was as dark and murky as the twilight surrounding him. Looking up into the sky, he could hardly make out the faint light of the moon slipping in and out of shifting cloud cover. There weren't any visible stars, nor would there be before sunrise came in an hour and a half.

The current was flowing south, as always, sending southward the frigid water of the North Pacific. This time of year, water temperature would be no warmer than fifty-five degrees Fahrenheit on a sunny day and might drop as low as forty-eight degrees at night, cold enough to send a fully-grown male athlete of typical body composition into a state of hypothermia in under twenty minutes, and kill him in a couple hours, if he was healthy and well-rested to begin with.

Drake walked northward along the shoreline a little ways, heading loosely in the direction of a nearby cluster of condominium buildings. He kept far enough inland to stay out of reach of the tide.

As far as he could tell, the waters were still choppy all the way up to the Hotel Del Coronado, situated exactly a nautical mile north of the BUD/S compound, its steadfast elegance in perfect position to remind each passing trainee just how luxurious his life wasn't. On a day like this, water conditions being what they were, even the well-trained eyes of his instructors wouldn't be able to track him through the water efficiently.

Drake looked at the time on his Casio G-Shock, the watch favored by many special warfare trainees for its durability and relative affordability: almost four o'clock. Some of the other early birds would be starting to stir now, preparing for the class's usual 0450 muster on the blacktopped parking lot outside the CBH generally referred to as 'the grinder.' He removed his shower shoes, clapping the sand off of them as he began strolling back southward.

2

Drake verified the number on his door: 317, and slid his electronic keycard through the lock several times before it finally registered. He opened his door in time to catch a glimpse of Jones, completely naked, urinating out the window onto whatever unsuspectingly rested below, an impressive feat for a man of his short stature. This was just one of many methods implemented in the constant attempts of the weary BUD/S trainees not to travel all the way down to the head on the first deck to urinate and risk expending the slightest bit more energy than absolutely necessary. Even if the class' barracks maintenance officer hadn't insisted that the second and third deck heads be closed for ease of pre-inspection cleaning, most of the trainees on those decks still wouldn't have wanted to expend the energy to climb out of bed and walk down the hall to reach them in the wee hours of the morning.

"What the hell is that?" said a muffled voice coming from the drying cages outside Drake's room.

"Hey, shitbag, quit pissing on my wetsuit!" yelled the same voice.

"My bad, bro," replied Jones sleepily as he stepped back from the window, taking care not to spill any amount of urine on the perfectly polished floor of their always-inspection-ready room. He noticed the light coming from the hallway and turned to greet his roommate.

"What up, Drake?" he said in the casually accented slang that had somehow succeeded in slipping through the cracks of four years of Academy finishing. He had managed to fake the same sense of polished refinement that emanated from those classmates of his who had come from far more privileged backgrounds, but here it was no longer necessary. He was now, like all the men around him, a diamond that would forever remain in the rough, the industrial grade variety too rugged to wear on an earring or necklace but perfect for edging the blade of a scalpel.

"Good morning, Sir," answered Seaman Drake, always insisting on maintaining perfect military bearing, despite the somewhat informal relationship of the officers, NCOs, and junior enlisted personal who all underwent the same treatment and training here at BUD/S. They lived in the same quarters, ran side by side in the soft sand, and dreamed the same dreams of IBS (inflatable boat: small) surf passages and the notorious first phase log PTs.

"How many times am I gonna have to tell you to relax, man? You know you don't have to keep callin' me 'Sir,'" Jones uttered through his grimacing as he peeled the bandage off his left ankle. The thin film of skin that had grown over a quarter-sized blister during the night came with it, releasing from the now-exposed abscess a mixture of blood and pus that proceeded to drizzle slowly downward.

"Aww, shit. Come give me a hand with this, will ya?"

asked Jones as he flipped on the light switch.

Drake removed a homemade, mix-and-match first aid kit from his wall locker and carried it over to Jones, now seated at the desk centered along the wall opposite their bunk bed structure. He placed a clean towel over part of the desk and gently propped Jones' leg onto it before beginning to rinse out the growing wound just above Jones' heel with hydrogen peroxide.

"Damn, that stings!" protested Jones as he tried his best not to show what many BUD/S instructors had come to refer to as the 'bitch face.'

"You would lessen the chafing against your skin by cutting out your boot's cardboard heel pad."

'Deheeling,' as it was called, was the simplest solution to the discomfort created by the overly-rigid support system of the Bates 922 combat boot, the standard issue footwear of today's SEAL trainees. Ideally, there would be time for the trainee to break in each new pair of boots he received at his own convenience, but BUD/S was a place that didn't reward consideration for individual conveniences and as much mileage as there was to be had on foot every day, it wasn't uncommon for a pair of boots to lose its tread within six weeks of issue, depending on the wearer's running style.

"Maybe I'll get to that this weekend, if I live through the week," said Jones, louder this time, completely failing to conceal the bitch face. Drake spread a fingertip's worth of Neosporin over the wound and covered it with a large bandage, securing the bandage to Jones' leg with a segment of athletic tape to prevent slippage throughout the day.

"Thanks for the help, Drake."

"Anytime, Sir."

"You ready for today's ocean swim?"

Of course he was ready for today's two-mile ocean swim. Drake, having been a state champion both years he was a member of the Malibu High School swim team, was easily the best swimmer in class 269, and everyone knew it. Besides, he had already passed Tuesday's ocean swim two days ago and therefore wouldn't need to pass another until phase two of training, which he didn't plan on reaching anyway. Come the day of '69's next phase-up, Seaman Apprentice Drake would be long gone, his name forgotten amongst the thousands of others to come and go over the years.

But, before he had time to answer, Drake was already out the door and on his way down to the head to shave, as he was every morning at exactly 0410. He still remembered clearly Instructor Stokley's visit to BUD/S Prep, Illinois approximately six weeks ago, in which he held a very short briefing on the expected conduct of the incoming BUD/S trainees.

'Listen up, assholes. You will shave EVERY day; not the night before, the morning OF,' had been his reply to Aviation Ordnanceman Second Class Dwayne's question of 'what should we do to prepare ourselves for first phase?'

AO2 Dwayne, class Assistant Leading Petty Officer, was one of those rare types who took more pride in being a Sailor than a SEAL trainee, and as such lacked the typical SEAL trainee sense of superiority over their non-special warfare counterparts that brought blanket loathing from the rest of the Navy down onto anyone who had ever left the BUD/S training pipeline. Nobody who hadn't personally looked through his records knew where he was from, as he'd always respond to inquiries about his origins by making some reference to CVN-65, the U.S.S.

Enterprise, aboard which he had been stationed since
shortly after his January 2002 enlistment. He had started
out swabbing decks and chipping paint as an undesignated Seaman, being given the opportunity to strike for the
Aviation Ordnance rating during the Enterprise's involvement in Operation Iraqi Freedom (originally Operation
Iraqi Liberation until the acronym O.I.L. was deemed
overly-appropriate by left-wing war protestors), for which
the carrier's primary role was air support. Observing a
slow-down in the advancement of said rating, he submitted his SEAL package upon the Enterprise's return to its
homeport of Norfolk, VA in late 2007, barely sneaking
into class 269 within a month of its completion of BUD/S
Prep. Now only two short years from fulfilling his current
contract, Dwayne fully intended to reenlist as a SEAL operator and continue pushing forward in his naval career.

As Drake opened the door to the head, now crowded
two to a showerhead and three to a sink with scantily-
clothed SEAL trainees, all rushing to get their faces
shaved and wounds cleaned before beginning the daily
grind all over again, he noticed a shallow pool of urine
and water forming underneath the four urinals on the far
wall. It was growing steadily as every urinal continued
to overflow. This phenomenon, as class 269's barracks
officer had observed, occurred when all four urinals were
flushed simultaneously and at least one urinal's drain-
age pipe was clogged with chewing tobacco, the drug of
choice among many SEAL trainees, especially those who
had been smokers before entering the pipeline. It would
probably be best to wait on taking a piss until he had to
hit the surf anyway, figured Drake. No matter how long

anybody has been at BUD/S, or how much they've heard about surviving cold water submersion, during surf immersion, or 'surf torture' as it is more commonly known, nobody ever has to be told that self urination is the surest way to not only warm yourself, but also put smiles on the faces of the men to your immediate left and right.

"Sid, what's up, man?" said a voice coming from one of the nearby stalls that was instantly identifiable as belonging to Seaman Brandon Clarke. Seaman Clarke was one of those guys who didn't have to do anything other than open his mouth to get guys thinking either 'how has that guy not DORed yet?' or just plain 'what the hell?' Clarke, although well built and in relatively good shape, had a face plump enough to create the illusion of pudginess. It was one of many traits that made him look not better, not worse, just more so.

Clarke had also been in Drake's boot camp division and was one of exactly two trainees from whom Drake felt comfortable hearing his first name, the other being Seaman Scott Driscoll, though Drake usually preferred that they address each other on a last name basis only during the workday.

"Mornin', Clarke," responded Drake in his usual flat tone, a tone that Clarke would have interpreted as conveying disinterestedness coming from anyone else. He knew better with Drake. The characteristic surface coldness he'd worn as long as any of his BUD/S classmates had known him was no more indicative of genuine apathy than any emotion he showed was indicative of genuine empathy.

"Drake, always so controlled, so fiercely concentrated. You're just so manly, like an animal, like a *man*imal!" Drake wasn't sure if it was Clarke's words or simply his twangy southern voice that was drawing concerned stares from a couple of nearby Sailors.

"Ha, thanks, I think. How's your family getting settled in?"

"They're doing alright, but we haven't unpacked anything other than our beds yet. Jamie is recovering really well from the birth. Sara still spends most of the day sleeping. I guess it's normal for a newborn. Thanks again for the blanket. Jamie loved it, and I'm sure Sara will too once she's old enough to appreciate the humor." Previously mentioned concerned Sailors returned to their own conversations and morning routines.

"No problem, I'll see you out on the grinder." Drake finished shaving his face, being careful not to nick himself, being more careful not to miss even the smallest hair on his face or neck. He wasn't about to put himself in a position to attract unnecessary negative attention from the instructors, not to say that there really exists any other kind of instructor attention.

Drake was in the stairwell now, heading back to his room, his anticipation of the day's events causing more and more adrenaline to flow through him as the usual morning feeling of drowsiness steadily faded away. He jumped the steps two, three, four at a time, habitually counting each in his head, "Six... seven... eight..." and then he was back on the third deck, proceeding towards his room.

"Good morning, Mr. Call," he said, quietly but clearly as he passed Lieutenant Junior Grade Call, '69's Assistant Officer in Charge.

"Morning, Drake," replied Call, in an equally professional tone. Everybody in the class knew it was only a matter of time before he replaced LTJG Vickers as the class OIC. He had formerly been an enlisted Sailor, and was now three years into his commission, during which he had made very few errors, and none to which he wouldn't admit freely.

Vickers, on the other hand, had much less practical leadership experience, in spite of having had more time in grade. He wasn't a bad man, but he didn't understand the worth of the enlistees or junior officers under him like Call did, or how to utilize them effectively. The son of a former SEAL Lieutenant Commander and the grandson of a retired SEAL Captain, Nathan Vickers was convinced that it was his duty, and generally acted as if it were his divine right to follow in their footsteps. It seemed obvious to everyone in class 269, with the exception of Vickers himself, that he'd applied for the program more because he believed his family expected it of him than because he desired, or was truly qualified, to lead Navy SEALs.

Drake arrived at his room, finding the door propped open by the deadbolt, and pushed it open, scanning the room as he entered. He didn't see Jones inside. He did see the American flag still mounted high on the wall to his left. It was the only item authorized to be displayed in the room, except, of course, for the thin strips of white athletic tape applied to each trainee's rack and locker, stenciled in black with his name. It had been Jones' idea to put up the flag.

It was now 0420. Drake quickly opened his locker and proceeded to dress himself, pants first, then socks, then boots, wrapping the laces once around his ankle before securing them with a square knot and tucking them, along with the legs of his woodland-style, camouflage BDU pants, into his boots.

"Pants, socks, boots, motherfuckers! You can do the rest on the fly, so from now on, you start getting dressed pants first, then socks, then boots," Instructor Peterson had told them three weeks earlier, on the first day on indoctrination.

"When all you whiny bitches go crying home to your mommies because you couldn't handle a little bit of cold water and a little bit of PT here at BUD/S, they better fucking be asking why you always put your pants on first, and then your socks, and then your boots!"

He made sure that every button of his pants was fastened before tucking in a brand new, white T-shirt, stenciled across the chest as well as the upper back with his name, in big, black, capital letters, the same as every other he had put on at the start of each day of BUD/S. He then donned his BDU blouse and green web belt with canteen. Again, he checked to make sure every button on his top was fastened, ID card and room key placed inside one sandwich-size zip-lock bag in the left breast pocket, soft cover folded and placed inside the right breast pocket, secured to his blouse by a segment of red line, canteen full to the cap so it made no noise when shaken, every piece neatly stenciled with his name.

As for the swimwear he would be using this afternoon, that was all waiting for him outside, locked in his seabag, hanging up in the first phase drying cage, compartment number 024. Drake removed the sleeping bag from atop his rack and folded it neatly before placing it on the top shelf of his locker. A sleeping bag, as he and many before him had discovered, was much more convenient to stow than a bunk bed was to make-up every morning. This was doubly true for trainees like Jones, who were too short to make their top bunk-beds themselves.

Drake took one last look at the hand written SEAL ethos hanging up on the inside of his wall locker door. It was the only item posted there. All trainees were required to have one present in their lockers at all times, and were also encouraged by the trainees of classes past to include pictures of their family members, particularly sisters, especially if they were attractive. Supposedly, it would help divert the instructors' attention from inspecting the rest of the room during inspections.

But Drake was the only surviving member of his family. His mother had died giving birth to him, her one and only child, and his father had been killed fifteen years later in a car collision not far from the BUD/S compound. Luckily for Drake, his birth had been on U.S. soil, albeit to parents who were both British nationals, so had been granted U.S. citizenship. He had also inherited British citizenship from his parents and, although it was necessary for him to renounce it to the U.S. government during his recruitment to obtain security clearance, he was still recognized as a citizen by the British government.

Drake shut and locked his locker, setting the dial of the combination lock to '0' before grabbing his hard cover, a green hard hat stenciled on either side with the number '269' as well as his name across the front and back. Since enlisting in the Navy several months before, Drake had become increasingly grateful to have a last name with relatively few letters, almost feeling pity for those poor bastards who would spend the rest of their careers writing 'CHRISTOPHERS' or 'MANGUAL-VELASQUEZ' on everything they owned. Satisfied that everything on his person and in his room was properly configured, he left the room and headed back down the hall, leaving the door bolted open for Jones.

Drake spotted Jones returning to their room to finish his own preparations just as he turned the corner to enter the stairwell again. It was 0430 now and Drake was joined by dozens of his classmates, rushing outside to join the rest of the class on the grinder outside the east entrance of the CBH.

"Boat-crew muster!" yelled voices all around him, calling the class into boat-crew formation, where each member of the class had been assigned to one of thirty-one, seven-man 'boat-crews,' arranged north to south in order of height, starting with the tallest, primarily for ease of achieving a speedy head-count and use during small group-oriented activities where height consistency among members was vital.

As he approached his own boat-crew, Boat-crew Two, Drake joined them in their bellowing, "Boat-crew muster!" passing the word as everyone in the class had repeatedly been instructed to do whenever a piece of information was put out.

"Boat-crew Two, up one: Drake," he said to Seaman Hernandez who was already standing by in position, and the word was passed up through the other members of the boat-crew to their boat-crew leader, Hospital Corpsman Third Class Phelps.

Phelps wasn't the typical SEAL trainee (if there is such a thing). He was tall and handsome and muscular, but not muscular in the usual bulky way of most of his classmates. He had more the slender build of a triathlete, making him an exceptional runner and swimmer. He didn't have quite the physical superstructure most candidates relied on to pull them through BUD/S' strength oriented evolutions, but what he lacked in mass he made up for in motivation.

This was Phelps' second try at BUD/S. He had been medically dropped during his first attempt nearly two years ago when he sustained a heart attack a few hours into Tuesday of Hellweek. This time around, most of his classmates, including Drake, considered him to be a shoo-in, and so far, he was more than meeting their expectations.

"That makes seven. Boat-crew Two, get down on a knee," ordered Phelps, taking a knee himself to signify that his boat-crew was 'up' (all members present).

All around him, boat-crews began to take knees one-by-one until at last only three remained standing. LTJG Vickers, class OIC, and Master-at-Arms Second-Class Kuslidge, a stocky, Colombian-American former left-tackle and now class 269's Leading Petty Officer, stood at the front of the formation, each armed with a clipboard, eagerly awaiting input from the three boat-crew leaders who still stood erect.

Vickers and Kuslidge, although technically the most senior trainees in their respective spectrums, were not even close to being the best choices for the leaders of this class. The two appeared, in both their physical aspects and their behavioral mannerisms, more like a carnie and his pet ape than like the Officer in Charge and Leading Petty Officer for a group of up-and-coming elite warriors. Some of the trainees suspected that their appointment might be part of yet another instructor scheme to make their lives more difficult than necessary.

Drake heard Ensign Greenwood, the leader of Boat-crew One and the tallest trainee in the class at six feet, eight inches tall in boots, call out from his right, "Boat-crew One, down one: Johnson, medical!" Then from his left, a little ways down the formation two other boat-crew leaders added, "Boat-crew Twelve, down two: Hill and Marshall, medical!" and "Boat-crew Fourteen, down one: Sanders, DOR!"

Kuslidge and Vickers hastily recorded the information on their clipboards. Vickers whispered something to Kuslidge before running to the north end of the formation where LTJG Call was awaiting him.

"STANDBY!" yelled a trainee from somewhere at the back of the formation. Before anyone had time to think, the entire class was on its feet, standing crisply at attention. The only times anybody ever called 'standby' were upon the arrival or departure of an instructor.

"I need two guys: one volunteer and a swim-buddy to go with him. Make it somebody with a car," Drake heard from behind the formation, in a voice he instantly identified as belonging to Instructor Stokley.

Stokley, like most members of the purely SEAL instructor staff, was a man not especially tall, nor built, nor good looking. The only physical features to separate him from any other Average Joe were his extensive tattooing, including two full sleeve collages and a white Trident on the back of his neck, and his extensive scarring, much of which had likely been sustained in the training he had undergone on his way to becoming a SEAL.

"Drake, you go. You've got a POV," said Phelps reflexively.

"Moving!" responded Drake as he turned and ran, full speed, to meet Stokley.

Stokley was dressed in the standard BUD/S instructor work uniform: Bates 922 boots, woodland-style BDU trousers, 'Blue and Gold' T-shirt, Oakley sunglasses, and woodland-style BDU cover.

Sewn onto the front panel of the starched-stiff octagonal cover was the rank insignia of a Petty Officer Second Class. It consisted of a 'Perched Eagle' usually referred to as the 'Crow' resting atop two downward-pointing chevrons. It matched the soft covers worn by the other instructors or trainees occupying the same pay grade.

"Moving!" yelled Seaman Leslie, a medical rollback from class 267, breaking apart from Boat-crew Five to join Drake.

Stokley eyed the stencil on Drake's BDU blouse before addressing him, "Okay, Drake, am I saying that right? Drake? There's not some weird gay French way of pronouncing it, is there?"

"It's just 'Drake,' Instructor Stokley." It was hard to keep from cringing as he said the words. Holding back whatever verbal retaliations he felt the urge to say to the taunting instructor was like trying to keep from spitting after finding half a worm in his apple.

"Good. Drake, something terrible has happened and I need you to fix it. We're out of coffee in the first phase office, so I need you to drive across the street to the coffee shop by the NEX and talk to the pretty blonde girl who works it and bring me back one cup of black coffee. Again, that's black coffee, with nothing in it but coffee, no sugar, no cream, no liquor, just coffee. Can you do that for me, Seaman Drake?"

"Hoo-yah, Instructor Stokley."

"Here's two dollars. This should cover it. Now go and bring it to the first phase office before your class leaves for chow."

"Hoo-yah, Instructor Stokley." Drake accepted the

money and took off at a run to collect his car keys from inside the CBH.

He returned a moment later to find Vickers giving the class a short brief on the plan of the day, even though everyone already knew exactly which evolutions they had scheduled: IBS Surf Passage, Mental Toughness Class with Master Chief Talbert followed by twenty minutes of 'Proctor Time,' and finally, Timed Two Mile Ocean Swim.

Drake ignored him as he and Leslie sprinted past the class, over the grinder, and out the front gate to his POV (privately owned vehicle), a gray 2007 Porsche 911 997 Turbo he had been wise enough to bring with him from home. POVs were easily the single best storage units for personal belongings here at BUD/S, especially contraband, because they could be kept on base but were off-limits to instructors as far as inspections were concerned.

Stokley caught a glimpse of him as he unlocked the door and climbed in. 'That's a nice car for a guy making fifteen hundred bucks a month,' he thought. He recognized it as being the same model as one he had crumpled in a collision a few years back, right after his own graduation from SEAL Qualification Training.

15JUN2005: One mile west of the intersection of Hillis St. with Spruce Ave., San Diego, CA.

"So, J.T., what are you going to spend your enlistment bonus on anyway?"

"You mean other than the massive bar tab we just ran up?

"Ha ha, yeah."

"Hell if I know. Does it even matter? We're Team guys now. That's all I'm worried about. You?"

"I'm trying to decide what color Mustang I'm gonna buy so I won't have to keep taking the duty truck every time I want to go

out. Speaking of bar tabs, you sure you don't want me to drive?"

"Taylor, shut the fuck up and go back to being the designated navigator."

"Aye, aye, SO3. Just try not to get us killed before I have time to collect my hard-earned sign-on incentive."

Stokley shuddered slightly at the image before returning his attention to the trainee he'd just put in charge of gathering his daily pick-me-up. What was his name? Drake, that's right. The name was familiar from somewhere. It nagged at his memory, but he couldn't place it. He continued to think about it as he disappeared into the first phase staff office.

"Four ranks to move, facing the north gate!" came the word from Kuslidge as he jogged up to join the OIC and AOIC.

"Four to move north!" spread the word southward through the class like wildfire as the trainees shifted into four columns of about fifty trainees each, still loosely organized into boat-crews.

The sound of two hundred pairs of 922s pounding on dry pavement spread throughout the compound as the class began its one-mile jog to the dining hall on the Naval Amphibious Base, located across the highway from BUD/S.

Drake returned to the compound and parked just as the class was passing through the front gate.

"Drake, I'll take that to the office for you. I've got to talk to Senior Chief before I head over to chow," said Jones as he jogged towards Drake.

"All yours, Sir." Drake handed off Stokley's coffee

and he and Leslie fell into place with the rest of the class.

Drake saw Seaman Branson, also of Boat-crew Two, break out of the row in front of him and fall back towards the center of the formation as he started to call cadence. He was often selected to call cadence for the class, because he had the lungs to yell all day long and the voice to make it sound like cadence should: confident, motivational, and, depending on the cadence, completely tasteless.

"Super-Man was a Man of Steel!"

"Super-Man was a Man of Steel..." echoed the class in response.

"But he Ain't no Match for a Navy SEAL!"

"But he Ain't no Match for a Navy SEAL..." The class continued to sing on as they passed through a stretch of soft sand, stirring up a sizeable dust cloud, slowly closing the distance between themselves and their much-desired breakfast.

Inside the perpetually cluttered first phase office, trainee service records, Men's Health magazines, and random pieces of exercise equipment were strewn about in no coherent manner. Atop some of the desks in the room, instructors had placed pictures of their wives or children or girlfriends, or their buddies' girlfriends. Many also had pictures of their own BUD/S and SQT graduations, and deployments they'd had in the past.

A few instructors were starting to get to work themselves, planning out how they would inflict the curriculum on the class today.

"It's a big class, Senior. If I'm not mistaken, there hasn't been one to make it to the fourth day of first phase with that many dudes before."

"That's right, Stokley," replied Senior Chief Marcus Grand indifferently. He was comfortably slouched back in the only chair in the office sturdy enough to support such a mountain of a man. His feet, clad in a dirty, though visibly well-shined beneath the film of dust, pair of 922s, rested atop the desk before of him. His beefy forearms were folded across a proportionately muscular chest.

In addition to a set of thickly-callused knuckles, the ring finger of his left hand was equipped with a heavy, silver ring. Super-imposed in gold over a Roman numeral 'VI' was the SEAL Trident logo. The ring, somewhat like Senior Chief Grand himself, was a relic left over from the days before SEAL Team Six had officially been dissolved and effectively replaced by the Naval Special Warfare Development Group or DEVGRU.

"You think it's gonna be a record breaker?" asked Stokley, his high-pitched voice sounding meek and weasely compared to that of the Senior Chief, which was every bit as low as the dull rumbling of the training group passing by their office, just beginning to cross Silver Strand Boulevard.

"I think it's too early to speculate. Who knows how many we're going to lose before the start of Hellweek, much less during Hellweek itself?"

'Hellweek' was the name given to the 132-hour period beginning the Sunday night after the third week of first phase, during which all remaining trainees would be put through a lengthy gauntlet of physical evolutions in rapid succession, pausing briefly to eat every six hours, but not being allowed to sleep more than a total of four hours throughout the entire event.

"What are you doing tonight after you finish up here,

Stokley?" inquired Grand, having been sure to keep an especially close eye on the junior instructor staff since BUD/S' command master chief left for his hometown of Ardmore, Oklahoma on leave two days earlier. No matter how mean or how tough any of these guys was, or how much shit he had been through, they were still Grand's responsibility for the time being.

"Probably just going to hit up the gym for a little while, and then go over to Mc P's with Dunn and Peterson," answered Stokley, somewhat hesitantly.

"Don't do anything stupid." Grand, like everyone else at this command, was well aware of the fact that Stokley had been assigned to his position as a BUD/S instructor immediately following his third DUI eight months ago, not to mention a steadily growing list of non-alcohol-related legal and ethical infractions. His judgment as an operator could no longer be trusted, but the Teams had put so much money into training him (as they had all SEALs) that they couldn't afford to throw him out of the special warfare community entirely.

"I won't, Senior," was the last thing he said before solemnly departing the staff office, but it couldn't have been more obvious that Stokley still was, and always would be 'that guy,' the one everybody knows, who can't ever seem to learn his lesson before it's too late...

As the class approached the galley, Kuslidge spotted a dark-skinned, medium-built man in sunglasses and a blue T-shirt with the words 'UDT/SEAL Instructor' stamped in gold over the left breast posted outside the entrance to the dining hall. He held his right fist over his shoulder, signaling the class to come to a halt.

"Chief Avilez!" he yelled back to the mass of the class now standing at attention behind him. Chief Juan Avilez was 269's first phase proctor, which was basically just a fancy way of saying that for seven weeks he would be the one to dish out most of their beatings, as well as most of their praises if they managed to earn any.

"Hoo-yah, Chief Avilez!" bellowed the class in response, loudly enough to be heard across the entire base.

"OIC, LPO!" barked Avilez, to no one in particular.

"OIC, LPO!" echoed the class.

"Moving," simultaneously from two voices near the front of the formation.

"Moving!" echoed the class again.

"You guys both have watches, right?"

"Hoo-yah, Chief," replied Kuslidge.

"Vickers?"

"Hoo-yah, Chief."

"Okay, what time is it?"

"0520, Chief."

"And what time is your first training evolution today?"

"IBS surf passage at 0630, Chief."

"That means you have over an hour to make sure every man in this class gets enough to eat that we don't have a relapse of yesterday's conditioning run. Do you know how many trainees fell out between the start of that run and the time the class arrived here for lunch immediately following said run?"

"Nineteen, Chief, all to medical," replied Vickers, inwardly proud of himself for not having failed to remember the number.

"Nineteen is right, and of those nineteen, two nearly died. By the time Donovan showed up at the clinic, his blood glucose level was so low he could barely stand upright and he had a core temperature of 90.7." Chief Avilez turned to face the class.

"I know all you pretty ladies are worried about maintaining your figures, but none of you are to exit this galley without a full stomach. Understood?"

"Hoo-yah, Chief Avilez!"

Chief Avilez pulled out his cell phone and began dialing a number as he started down the street back towards the BUD/S compound. Several trainees relaxed noticeably as the SEAL Chief's attention shifted off of the class.

"You all heard him! Start falling in from the front; use both chow lines once you get inside! Swim-buddy assignments for today's two-miler will be posted at the entrance!" Vickers announced, not sounding especially authoritative.

Drake, being in Boat-crew Two and already at the front of the formation, was one of the first to enter. He decided he'd check his swim-pair assignation on the way out and avoid the worst of the traffic jam of overly-curious trainees that was sure to occur. As he broke ranks to head inside, he dropped his hard cover on top of HM3 Phelps', located about ten yards east of the door.

3

Last week's hijacking incident is just one of many in recent years indicating the United States' growing need for Special Forces teams to combat a new kind of enemy on a much smaller scale than those encountered in previous eras. Currently, all four branches of the United States Armed Forces have been upgrading their small-scale tactical capabilities, with the Navy continuing to lead the way in the recruitment of candidates for these programs, having stated that it intends to increase the total number of Navy SEAL operators from the mere four-hundred that were on active duty in years past to over 2,500 by the year 2010. This dramatic increase in numbers will not only increase the opportunities for the traditional applications of the Special Forces, but also increase the United States' ability to employ the Special Forces to train its allies to help in the fight against our enemies. This tactic, referred to as 'Indirect Warfare,' has been a

major focus of Admiral Eric Olson since he
became, last July, the first Navy SEAL ever
to hold the position of Commander of the
United States Special Operations Command,
or SOCOM.

Drake turned away from the television to face Seaman
Brown, seated across from him, who had begun
to say something hardly intelligible over a mouthful of
scrambled eggs.

"...but I guess that's why they're handing out forty-
thousand dollar signing bonuses, right?"

"Hell yeah it is, forty thousand good reasons not to
DOR!" Seaman Apprentice Gilbert reached across the
table to give Drake a high-five.

Drake did not respond to the gesture.

"You know as well as I do that the twenty-eight thousand dollars or so your forty will be worth after taxes and
inflation sixty-plus weeks from now isn't nearly enough
to keep anyone here. The guys who make it, make it
because they want to be Navy SEALs," Drake stated in
as much a condescending tone as a very insulted Gilbert
had ever heard, like a mother trying to explain the most
obvious of truths to a four-year-old.

"And who told you that? Your Porsche?"

The Porsche had been intended by Drake's father to
be a graduation gift for completing his third and final year
at Malibu High School when he purchased it two and a
half years earlier. However, Drake Senior had barely managed to leave the San Diego dealership when he was hit
passing through an intersection by a lifted F-350 pick-up
truck, the driver of which had run the red light. He was

killed almost instantly, the car technically 'totaled' as well, but Drake had insisted on having it fully restored.

"Maybe it was your wife's mustache," Drake sneered as Gilbert regretted, yet again, having disclosed the details of his wife's (a fellow Sailor he'd met at boot camp and somehow been convinced to marry) last personnel inspection, during which she had received a demerit for 'not being sufficiently clean-shaven.'

Gilbert rose to his feet, red-faced with anger and humiliation, and started to circumvent the large galley table, heading towards Drake. By now, several trainees from nearby tables had begun to catch on to their argument and were staring in anticipation of a fight.

"Gilbert, we all know you aren't going to do anything. Drake could beat your ass without getting out of his seat. Sit down and save it for BUD/S." Phelps was right. In fact, as long as Gilbert's Sasquatch of a wife wasn't around to help him, there were very few able bodied men, much less strapping young SEAL trainees at their physical peaks, who weren't capable of mopping the floor with him.

"Whatever, HM3." Gilbert paused briefly then returned to his seat, still glaring at Drake, who was now staring off into space somewhere, having long since lost interest in him, much like Gilbert had seen his cat, Poe, do countless times.

As Drake finished off a second glass of guava juice, he thought back to the police report on his father's accident (or 'murder' as he considered it) his insurance company had sent him a couple months after the fact.

Party #1 (P-1, Jonathon T. Stokley) was driving Vehicle #1

(V-1, Red 2001 Ford F-350) eastbound on Hillis St. in the middle lane at an undetermined speed. Party #2 (P-2, Derek N. Drake) was driving Vehicle #2 (V-2, Gray 2007 Porsche 911) northbound on Spruce Ave. in the middle lane at approximately 45 mph. V-1 failed to come to a halt when facing a red light and passed through the intersection of Hillis/Spruce, colliding with V-2. V-1 did not stop to render aid. V-1 fled the scene. P-1 and Passenger identified at a later date.

Jonathon Stokley, at that time Special Warfare Operator-Third Class Stokley and a recent graduate of SEAL Qualification Training (the last stop in the SEAL training pipeline before receiving the golden Trident pin worn by all Navy Special Warfare Operators) wasn't identified as being the driver of said duty pick-up truck until nearly three weeks later. He had fled the scene of the incident and, with the help of third-phase BUD/S instructor Chief Grand, who happened to be the watch Command Duty Officer on duty at the time, managed to dispose of the duty vehicle's checkout log before it could be inspected.

By the time the legal authorities had been able to piece together enough witness descriptions and video footage taken from traffic cameras to identify Stokley, he had already been sent on his first deployment with SEAL Team 3 to a classified location in the Middle East, and was un-recallable. Chief Grand's involvement was still unknown to anyone other than Stokley, and Stokley's best friend at the time, who had been in the truck with him when the collision occurred.

Drake hadn't felt especially discouraged. As the bereaved survivor in a family whose members had a way of dying long before their time, he wouldn't have been alright with justice getting to Stokley before he did, and eventually Stokley and his platoon would return to the San Diego area for the six month stand-down period that followed every deployment. So he waited, ever so patiently, until the opportunity for vengeance on the man who was to blame for taking away the only other Drake Sidney had ever known would present itself.

He got his lucky break sooner than expected when, one day last summer while visiting a friend at the University of San Diego, he spotted Instructor Hodges at a dorm party. He instantly recognized Hodges' face as matching that he'd seen in the local papers not long before, as well as in the collision report. In the report it had been labeled: V-1 Passenger. No official statement had been provided by him at any time after the collision.

Looking back, it was difficult to remember how hard it had been not to assault Hodges right then and there, disregarding any consequences of killing him in view of dozens of witnesses. 'Never attack anyone in anger,' his father had taught him at a young age, 'If you have to engage in a confrontation, don't let it be at a time when you're emotionally compromised.'

20JUL2007: Maher Hall, University of San Diego, San Diego, CA.
　　"Thanks for offering but I don't drink."
　　"I never thought I'd meet a SEAL who didn't drink."
　　"What makes you think I'm a SEAL?"
　　"You're wearing a Navy SEALs T-shirt."
　　"Plenty of guys wear Navy SEAL T-shirts, especially in this town."
　　"The only guys who would wear one with a pair of 922s are real SEALs. The trainees who get issued the same boots know better than to parade around town in anything displaying a Trident

before they actually get pinned."

"That's better spotting than I would have expected from the average college kid."

"Even the average college kid about to sign a contract to go to BUD/S?"

"Especially the average college kid about to sign a contract to go to BUD/S. What do you want from me?"

"I saw a picture of you and one of your friends in the newspaper, taken last Tuesday at the American Cancer Foundation half-marathon and didn't find your name, but couldn't help read that you're an instructor."

"First of all, Jonathon Stokley is not a friend of mine, not by a long-shot. And second, I've got better things to be doing than entertaining some wannabe SEAL punk looking for the secret solution to BUD/S. I'll answer one question and then you're going to leave this party, one way or another."

"Ok, I've got a question for you. Did you ever forgive Stokley for taking away any chance you'll ever have for becoming a real SEAL?"

Drake had just completed his freshman year at Stanford University when he notified his academic guidance counselor that he had been overcome by an 'overwhelming sense of patriotism' and desire to serve his country.

"Well isn't that just wonderful, Hon?" was all she had said in response before disenrolling him from the next semester's courses. Drake was barely seventeen years old but had been legally emancipated immediately following his father's death at the age of fifteen, claiming financial self-sufficiency upon his inheritance of nearly twelve million dollars' worth of stocks, bonds, gold and European sports cars so was fully capable of volunteering for military service.

The majority of those assets had remained exactly as they were when he inherited them until his enlistment into the Navy, at which point he had chosen to consolidate everything but the cars into one of two bank accounts for reasons of financial simplicity during a period when he wouldn't have enough time to micromanage it all efficiently. The half-dozen cars, all products of companies whose names ended with vowels with the exception of Derek Drake's own personal favorite, an antique Aston Martin, were under the care of a family friend who owned a restoration and body shop in London.

Into the first of the two accounts, opened at a local Bank of America, Drake had deposited exactly $100,000, at that time the maximum amount insurable by the FDIC. It was one of his father's (and therefore inevitably one of Drake's own) obsessions to maintain ready access to more money than one should ever need on short notice, but so far he hadn't used a single penny of it, having spent two months of his enlistment in basic training without the opportunity and the rest of his limited time in service subsisting off his Navy 'paycheck' for any necessary expenses. These were few since food and housing were covered by the American taxpayer.

The other of the two accounts was considerably more complicated. Technically, the account itself was owned by a Panamanian-based bearer share corporation (established solely for the purpose of maintaining said account in a Panamanian-based bank), the lone share holder of said corporation being authorized exclusive access to the entirety of the corporation's assets and therefore the account's contents. This lone 'bearer' was, of course, completely anonymous, even to the Panamanian government, and was, of course, Sidney Drake. Formally establishing such a corporation, although not requiring disclosure of any means of identifying the bearer (as such a requirement would completely defeat the purpose of establishing a bearer share corporation), did require the signatures of three nominee directors, or place-holder employees who in no way had claim to any corporate assets because they bore no company shares. Fortunately for Drake and the share bearers of the other 400,000 Panamanian bearer share corporations currently reinforcing the nation's reputation as 'the new Switzerland,' three nominee directors could be made available by whichever legal firm assisted the bearer in creating the corporation, and did not need to know the identity of the bearer themselves. The only actual expenses incurred during the process were an annual tax paid to the Panamanian government in the amount of $300, a minimal one-time fee (generally less than the tax) paid for the signatures of the nominee directors, and whatever the difference in interest was for deposited money that wasn't invested elsewhere, which wouldn't necessarily be negative. In either case, Drake had decided it would be worth the stagnation to know precisely in what state his family fortune perpetuated during his stint as a Sailor, particularly that it would be outside the grasps of either of the countries in which he held citizenship, and to ensure that it would be readily available to him when he needed it.

Right now, the physical bearer share, key to roughly ten million dollars of Drake family money, was folded up into the owner's manual of the Porsche. Drake trusted that it would be safe enough there, within the BUD/S compound under the guard of the U.S. Navy SEALs and SOCOM, until it came time for him to check out and move on.

§

The volume level in the galley had consistently been at a dull roar. The two hundred or so BUD/S trainees and few dozen SWCC trainees were awake enough to converse, but still so obviously worn down from the last few weeks that nobody really wanted to talk except to discuss those matters immediately relevant to their training. Some trainees preferred to savor their final hour of dryness in silence, knowing that when they returned to the galley at lunchtime, they'd be sitting in their seats soaking wet, ankles, armpits, and neck chafed bloody, their scalps rubbed raw from carrying their IBSs overhead, and covered in so much sand it would be impossible to keep from ingesting some of it.

"'69, feet!" shouted MA2 Kuslidge from the southwest corner of the dining hall.

"Feet!" repeated Drake reflexively, along with the rest of the class.

"Here we go again. Yet another day of fine commando training begins," said Seaman Clarke as he joined Drake on their way over to the exit.

"Don't start without me," Drake said somewhat sarcastically, "I still need to check my swim pair."

Drake glanced at the first sheet posted in the foyer of main dining hall. Near the top of the list, he read:

Swim Pair 012/106 – SN De la Cruz / SA Draek

Drake knew that whichever of their class officers made up this list was every bit as worn down as the rest of the class after having had almost four weeks of grueling screening, one beat-down after another, but he still couldn't comprehend how a guy who failed to catch his own typos ever expected to have enough attention to detail to make it all the way through BUD/S, much less survive downrange.

His swim-buddy, De la Cruz was one of the class' better swimmers considering that he had no formal competitive swimming background. The popular belief amongst his fellow trainees was that most of the swim training he'd done had been the ninety miles or so between his hometown and Key West.

Because of his very limited knowledge of English, or maybe just his reluctance to discuss the matter, few people actually knew the truth about De la Cruz' background except that he was obviously Cuban by ethnicity.

Nobody really cared. From the day each SEAL trainee arrived at this particular training command until the day he left, by whatever means, the beast that is BUD/S would treat them exactly as equals, regardless of race, religion, rank, age, or any other distinguishable attribute. The only factor that could make one man better than another in this place was how badly he wanted to slay that beast.

Drake stumbled outside and joined his teammates in calling the class to boat-crew formation. He saw Phelps' hand in the air, displaying two fingers, at the north end of the mass of trainees gathering on the sidewalk and started to jog over, collecting his hard cover on the way.

"Boat-crew Two, up one: Drake," he said as he took a knee behind Phelps and Gilbert.

"Boat-crew Two, up one: Driscoll," he heard as Seaman Driscoll fell into place immediately behind him.

Drake and Driscoll, both standing six feet, three inches tall in boots and weighing in at a lean two hundred pounds plus, had been the two biggest, two fittest members of their boot camp division. They had, however, been on opposite poles of the age spectrum, Driscoll having turned thirty-three over winter exodus. Even here at BUD/S, Drake and Driscoll retained their status as the youngest and oldest trainees, respectively.

He saw Phelps glance over his shoulder and count by twos the six other members of his boat crew before taking a knee himself.

"Hey, old man, you look like you're movin' a little slower than usual today," said Drake as he watched Driscoll begin to massage his right knee.

"My ITB's been all jacked up this week, and there's no chance I'm going to risk a med-roll to get it looked at, at least not until after Hellweek." Driscoll was obviously in pain, but he had a good point about not wanting to get rolled yet. If he could hold out until they finished Hellweek, he would get put on 'BSRB' (Brown-Shirt Rollback, a reference to the brown undershirts that post-Hellweek trainees wore in lieu of the white T-shirts they had worn until they completed Hellweek) hold until class 270 caught up to him a couple months later. If not, he would have to repeat all three weeks of indoctrination and three days of first-phase that he had already endured.

The pain in the Iliotibial Band, or ITB, was one of the most common overuse injuries sustained in both BUD/S Prep and BUD/S. It was often said jokingly that ITBS really stood for 'I Tried BUD/S' Syndrome.

"If you're up from this morning's muster, get down!" directed Vickers from the west end of the formation. All boat-crew leaders were now kneeling.

"Four ranks to move, facing west."

"Four to move west!" The class rose as a unit and gathered into roughly four ranks on the street outside the dining facility, some trainees moving faster than others, most limping to one side or the other. The class had already lost nearly seventy members since the start of indoctrination twenty-four days ago, the plurality of medical drops due to injuries of the lower extremities.

"Moving," said a muffled voice at the front of the formation.

"Moving!" rippled the word eastward through the class as they began to trot back to the special warfare compound, nearly a mile away.

Drake, now at the back of the formation, would suffer the worst of the accordion effect which inevitably developed during any 'coordinated' full-class movement over uneven terrain. It just wasn't possible for all two hundred trainees to maintain their spacing perfectly for the duration of the run, but it would be much less of an issue for any remaining trainees one month from now, when half the class had washed out.

There was no cadence being called, but Drake could make out HM3 Gonzales' voice up ahead, speaking to MA2 Corbin, '3PO' (third most senior enlistee, directly below the ALPO in the class' chain of command).

"Hoy, Moolie, how long does it take a black lady to shit?" Gonzales, although one hundred percent Mexican by ethnicity, had been raised from birth in Massachusetts, and his accent, in conjunction with his skin color, had earned him the nickname 'Boston Beaner.' Gonzales also had the rare talent of being able to offend almost everyone around him, almost every time he opened his mouth.

"Longer than it takes you to DOR, I bet," said Corbin

in a voice that seemed much too high for a man of his large stature and much too feminine for a man a few weeks out of a deployment in Afghanistan.

"Nine months!"

The responses of the surrounding trainees ranged from subtle snickering to roaring, hooting laughter, to one look of complete and utter confusion by Seaman Paul, a native of Utah and the class' resident devout Mormon, not to be confused with Seaman Apprentice Paul, who claimed to be a non-practicing Mormon, but only to have at his disposal the obligation to go on Mission as justification for discharge from the Navy, should he be dropped from SEAL training. Unless the drop was for medical reasons, in which case junior enlistees were guaranteed by contract the option of separation from the Navy, they would likely be shipped out to some less desirable, less prestigious post in the event of a premature release from training.

Drake remained silent, rehearsing in his mind over and over again the procedures for rigging his uniform during surf passage.

Unblouse boots. Tuck-in BDU top. Remove web belt and hard cover, placing web belt in boat-crew formation, encircling hard cover. Remove canteen from web belt and place in right BDU trouser leg pocket. Place zip-lock bag containing ID card and room key into canteen pouch. Don life vest and soft cover. Ensure soft cover secured to BDU blouse by red line. Ensure all life vest clips clipped, all zippers zipped and tucked-in, and all buttons buttoned.

By now, the class had begun crossing Silver Strand Boulevard, reentering the BUD/S compound through the main gate just outside the NEX Surf-Mart, each trainee giving a 'Hoo-yah' as he passed through the intersection.

"Clear!" yelled AO2 Dwayne, the last man to cross. His voice was clearly audible all the way up to the front of the formation. It was powerful and deep, the kind that made for good cadence calling. It suited a man of his particular stature and build. Dwayne was about six feet, four and boasted a shoulder girdle whose development would rival that of a professional wrestler. Drake had wondered what practical use such excessive muscle-boundness might serve. Hauling around 'aviation ordnance,' he supposed.

"Clear!" from the rest of the class.

At the front of the formation, out of Drake's view, Mr. Vickers was instructing Kuslidge to prepare the class for their first evolution of the day: IBS surf passage.

"Have them rig for sea, then ground their gear in boat-crew formation along the north wall of the drying cages, Boat-crew One to the west."

"Sir, do you want them to take care of last minute IBS issues and start heading over the berm?"

Vickers checked his watch: 0612, eighteen minutes until they had to be lined up in formation over the berm, BDUs and IBSs rigged for sea. The day hadn't even started yet and time was already running short.

"We don't have any time to spend patching and re-inflating right now. That should have been taken care of last night. No additional maintenance is to be performed unless it's an emergency."

The body of the Inflatable Boat: Small consists of a one-foot diameter primary inflation tube around a semi-rigid rubber hull, with two large inflation tubes running port-to-starboard inside the boat, all of the above black, and one smaller, yellow inflation tube which also runs about the same perimeter as the primary tube. The IBS is outfitted with seven handles, three on each side and one in the rear for the coxswain. These are used to transport the boat in the hanging 'low carry' position as well as for stabilization when the boat is placed atop its crew members' heads in the 'head carry' position.

"Yes, Sir." Kuslidge glanced over his shoulder as he began putting out the word.

Drake tried to take in the information being passed back as it came to him in waves.

"Rig for sea when you reach the drying cages!" from up ahead.

"Rig for sea when you reach the drying cages..." rippled the word through the formation.

"Ground gear in boat-crew formation, One to the west!"

"Ground gear in boat-crew formation, One to the west..."

"Grab boats and form it up on the beach!"

"Grab boats and form it up on the beach..."

All members of the class began accelerating in unison, but at such inconsistent rates that they had effectively broken ranks and become a mob, some moving at a dead sprint in the direction of the barracks.

"Well, that's not good," said a nearby trainee as he looked in the direction of the bumbling, fumbling horde surging into the drying cages fifty yards ahead.

"What are we supposed to do about it?" asked another trainee from somewhere behind Drake.

"Only one thing we can do: try and catch up. Hooyah!" yelled the trainee at the top of his lungs as he took off after the rest of the class.

Drake was already two steps ahead of him, and moving as fast as he could in the direction of his own boat-crew as he began simultaneously tucking in his blouse and removing his web belt, hoping to save himself every extra second possible.

Inside the first phase staff office, Senior Chief Grand was just finishing filing HM3 Sanders' DOR paperwork, a process that lasted only minutes from start to finish. The mass flow of trainees out of the program made an efficient out-transfer process a necessity. To remove himself from the SEAL training pipeline, only three things were required from the trainee. First was an oral declaration of desire to discontinue training, which was almost always presented informally during a training evolution. Next, a reason for leaving, usually something along the lines of 'I'm too cold' or 'I'm too bad at running/swimming/shining my boots, etc.' The third and final step was:

DING! DING! DING!

Grand heard the bell outside his office sound for the thirteenth time since '69 began first phase only seventy-four hours earlier. The ringing was immediately followed by the clap of yet another 269 hard cover joining the twelve already lined up along the grinder's east edge.

'What is it that makes so many guys quit this place?' Grand thought to himself as he tried to remember his own trip through BUD/S more than two decades ago. After everything he had accomplished since, all the hardships he had endured on deployment, nothing that happened in BUD/S even seemed worthy of mention anymore. There had, of course, been deaths here before, but those that were considered 'training related' were few and far between, flukes by inexperienced, often disobedient trainees. In reality, the course of instruction of BUD/S, although intense, was so carefully plotted out, so closely monitored, that the total number of training-related deaths among students was by far the lowest of any of the military's training commands, especially those belonging to the special warfare community. And, as far as he knew, not a single instructor had ever died during a training evolution while stationed at (or 'sentenced' to) BUD/S.

A knock on his open door startled him slightly as he surrendered his train of thought for the meantime, quickly regaining situational awareness.

"Did I spook you, Senior Chief?" Instructor Dunn asked as he entered the room, sunglasses on, Styrofoam coffee cup/spittoon in hand, as always.

"Not at all," said Senior Chief, trying more to convince himself than Dunn. He really was getting complacent these days, having spent too many years out of the game and at a desk. He'd have to fix that if he was going to keep pace with these young guys. "What's on your mind?"

"Nothing much, just thought I'd stop by before the guys and I head out to watch the fun. Surf's lookin' really big out there. I bet we see every boat-crew get tossed at least once." Dunn always sounded enthusiastic when he talked about work, almost as enthusiastic as he sounded when he talked about his partying. It was rumored that the day he finished boot camp, when all his buddies had gotten tattoos of anchors on their forearms and shoulders, he had gotten a tattoo three inches below his belly button that read 'Welcome Aboard!' It was also rumored that the day he finished SEAL training, when all his buddies had gotten tattoos of Tridents across their chests or backs, he had gotten one drawn about three inches below his belly button to conceal the 'Welcome Aboard!' tattoo.

"It's 0635. Did the class actually form up in time today?" Senior Chief inquired hopefully, but doubtfully. Rarely did a class fall into an efficient rhythm fast enough to make all their first phase evolutions on time, especially a class this size, and so far, '69's rhythm had been everything but efficient.

"...everybody drop down..." they heard Chief Avilez' voice say from somewhere off in the distance.

"Doesn't sound like it. I'd better go give Chief a hand," Dunn said as he stood up.

"Alright, why don't you throw the drying cages while you're out there? Mix things up a little. We'll see who hasn't stenciled all his gear yet."

"Will do, Senior." Dunn turned and left, making an obvious point of closing the door on the way out.

'Great,' thought Grand as he breathed a heavy sigh. 'I'm barely over the hill and my own staff is already starting to pamper me. What was I thinking about? Oh, right. The BUD/S instructor staff has never sustained a casualty, at least not yet.'

4

The entire class hovered in the 'leaning rest,' the 'up' push-up position. There was stray gear strewn about all over. At least half the trainees were between uniforms, rigged neither for surf passage nor for regular activity. Of the three boat-crews that had managed to rig fully, none had actually made it over the berm with their IBS yet. It was the perfect picture of disorganization and at the very center of it, surveying expressionlessly, stood Chief Avilez.

"OIC, LPO," he demanded loudly but calmly.

"OIC, LPO!" echoed the class, many trainees yelling desperately at the tops of their lungs, already straining to maintain their leaning rests.

"Moving!" came Kuslidge's voice from somewhere inside the drying cages.

"Moving!" shouted Vickers, currently with his boat-crew near the bottom of the barracks-side of the berm.

Both candidates began to bear-crawl on all fours, working their way through the labyrinth of scattered trainees toward Avilez. They were careful not to come within six feet (the minimum acceptable standoff distance between candidates and instructors) of him before stopping and returning to the leaning rest.

Avilez looked down at them, his eyes hidden behind a pair of Oakleys, maybe angry, maybe disappointed, maybe just wondering if the girl he'd seen drive by him in her red Corvette last night had been wearing any underwear.

"Sir," Avilez paused briefly as Vickers cocked his head up in an attempt to make eye contact.

"Hoo-yah, Chief."

"Your inability to organize and lead this class is going to tear it apart before anyone here even reaches Hellweek. So far, your class has a sixty percent failure rate on personnel inspections and a seventy-five percent failure rate on room inspections. You continue to arrive late for training evolutions. You aren't communicating well with your class LPO. Do you know how I know you aren't communicating with your class LPO?"

"Negative, Chief." There was a trace of strain in Vickers' voice as he flexed his abdominal muscles to keep his waist from sagging.

"Because, sir, when I dropped you down five minutes ago, he was still stuck in the drying cages half-naked and you were already about to cross the berm. You can't be communicating if you aren't with each other. As long as the two of you are in command of this class, you are to remain together at all times. We can't have the two class leaders running around in opposite directions, giving the class incongruous orders, failing to maintain consistency in muster records." Avilez turned his attention to Kuslidge.

"Kuslidge."

"Hoo-yah, Chief."

"Kuslidge, I'm going to let you in on a little secret."

"Hoo-yah, Chief."

"Although this may be hard to believe, you're class 269's LPO. Vickers and the other class officers can plot and plan all they want but when it comes down to making shit happen, that's your job. Your failure to effectively motivate the men under you couldn't be more obvious." Avilez took a step back from Vickers and Kuslidge and spoke to the trainees as a class.

"As you can all clearly see, there are three boat-crews just about to cross the berm. They are proof that you've all had plenty of time to get yourselves squared away and get moving. The rest of you are still piled in the drying cages with your heads up your asses, taking your sweet time, thinking I won't notice when you slack off. I'm not just talking to the class Crows either. Not having any chevrons is no excuse to perform to a lower standard. BUD/S, like the real world, only has one standard."

Avilez turned back to Kuslidge.

"If somebody in your class isn't pulling their weight, *you* motivate them. If one boat-crew continues to fall behind, *you* motivate them. If half your fucking class can't get dressed and get lined up on that beach, *YOU* motivate them!" Avilez jogged towards the berm, weaving in and out of the hundreds of trainees still hovering over the deck. He ran part way up the berm and turned around to address the class one last time.

"OIC, LPO, get up and get your class formed up beyond the berm before the rest of my staff gets here!"

"Hoo-yah, Chief!" both shouted in unison, springing to their feet as Kuslidge began directing the class.

"'69, recover!"

The entire class jumped to its feet. Those who were

already rigged rushed to their IBSs and began running towards the surf at full speed.

"Kuslidge, I'll get Dwayne to cover you. Go get dressed and get back out here. ALPO!"

"ALPO!" shouted the remaining trainees together without slowing their preparations.

"Moving!" returned AO2 Dwayne, donning his life-vest as he ran over to meet Vickers at the entrance to the drying cages.

"Dwayne, as soon as Kuslidge gets out here, we're going over the berm to get the class lined up. Keep the stragglers moving and make sure the drying cage gets locked when the last man leaves. Do a quick sweep of the downed gear to make sure it at least looks like it's in boat-crews and then haul ass down to the surf and get in your boat-crew."

"Hoo-yah," was all Dwayne said before beginning to issue commands to the forty or so trainees still dressing out in the drying cages.

"If you're already done, help your buddy! You can get zippers and buttons on the fly! Make sure every piece of gear is stowed properly. Move fast but don't get careless!"

By now, Drake had donned all the necessary pieces of equipment and was sprinting southward parallel to the wall of the drying cages, almost to his boat. The other members of his boat-crew were close behind and the bunch started taking their boat down from storage compartment two as soon as they arrived. They were still fumbling around with buttons and zippers as their IBS wobbled uneasily out of its storage rack, nearly landing on Phelps and Driscoll in the process.

"This thing's already going flat. It must have been

leaking all night!"

"Don't worry about it. There's no time to fix it now. Boat-crew Two, prepare to up boat," ordered Phelps.

"Up boat!" All members of the boat-crew, three on each side and Phelps in the rear, hoisted the boat up in unison and let it rest atop their heads as they started to run towards the berm. They were fortunate to all be about the same height. Those boat crews with greater height discrepancies always had trouble distributing the weight evenly and 'comfortably' amongst their members.

In less than thirty seconds they were over the berm, heading towards their place at the north end of the formation. Almost every other boat-crew was already in position, standing at attention beside their IBSs. Inside each were seven small wooden paddles, covered with fresh coats of black paint.

Drake and Driscoll, the forward-most trainees of their boat-crew, occupied the 'One' slots under their boat, with Gilbert and Branson in the 'Two' slots, and lastly Brown and Hernandez at the rear of the boat, Phelps centered between them. Drake slowed steadily to a halt as they approached their place in formation and allowed the back end of the IBS to swing around so that they would be in position facing the surf.

"Prepare to down boat. Down boat." They set their IBS down gently into the soft stand and quickly checked over their own equipment, making sure all zippers, buttons, covers, etc. were properly secured before finally coming to attention.

At last, Drake could relax for a minute and catch his breath. He peered out into the surf zone, unusually large waves still rolling in at a consistent rate. Around him, he could see in the faces of all his classmates that at that moment, everyone was thinking the exact same thought: 'my Itty Bitty Ship is going to be the one that gets tossed today and I'm going to get an oar to the face and lose some teeth, or an eye, or some combination of the two, and it'll leave a really cool scar.'

Boat-crew One pulled up alongside Drake's own, just far enough apart that both boat-crews had room to drop down and 'push 'em out' in the case of a spontaneous remediation session, which was bound to come sooner or later. Their boat was the last in the class to fall into place. The instant it touched down, Drake heard Instructor Hodges' voice come at him from somewhere behind the class, sounding through a megaphone.

"Coxswains, report!"

Drake turned his head slightly to catch a glimpse of Hodges standing atop the berm, eyeing the trainees before him like an eagle might survey a nest of some lesser prey species as he decided which one was going to be the first course of dinner.

Hodges wasn't like the other instructors. He had become a 'Blue and Gold' right out of SQT after receiving a head injury that prevented him from ever being deployed, so he was the only instructor on the staff without field experience, but he'd been at BUD/S longer than any of the others, having pushed over a dozen classes. His experience with both training and screening candidates earned him a reputation as the resident 'expert' as far as instructors were concerned. He had seen so many thousands of potentials pass through his gauntlet that he had developed a keen eye for spotting those that weren't going to make it, though he rarely shared his insights with the other instructors.

There was, however, something else about him that

separated him from the others. It was something that nobody seemed quite able to put his finger on. Maybe it had to do with the strange combination of apathy towards the astronomical attrition rate of BUD/S and the obvious lengths to which he went to ensure that every single evolution was administered flawlessly. To the other instructors it seemed strange, even in this setting, that one could appear to commit so completely, so blindly to his trainees, and at the same time be so unemotional about their success or failure.

What they never really understood about Hodges was that he hadn't committed a day of his life to helping any of the candidates under him. Hodges was a professional committed to the paycheck and as such insisted on providing a service that was every bit as consistent and reliable as that paycheck. He never dropped a beat. He never missed a detail. He never made a mistake.

"Coxswains, report!" shouted everyone in the class at the top of their lungs, still not matching the volume produced by Hodges.

In a matter of seconds, thirty-one boat-crew leaders, each armed with an oar, were standing at parade rest atop the berm, out of sight of the rest of the class. Instructor Hodges began carefully inspecting them, one-by-one, starting from the south end of their line-up.

"Seaman Jackson, Boat-crew Thirty-One, reporting," stated the shortest man ever to be accepted into the SEAL training pipeline as he sharply came to attention before Instructor Hodges.

"Seaman Jackson, huh?"

"Hoo-yah, Instructor Hodges!"

"Seaman Jackson, how tall are you?"

"Five feet, Instructor Hodges."

"That sounds about right. Tell me, five foot tall Seaman Jackson, are you the boat-crew leader of Thirty-One because you're the senior man or because you're the shortest man?"

Jackson did not respond. He stood crisply at attention, hoping Hodges wouldn't spend much time on him before moving on to his next victim. Fortunately for Jackson, before there was time to answer, Hodges noticed that a few trainees up the line stood Seaman Richardson with no oar in hand.

"Hold that thought, Frodo."

Jackson breathed a short sigh of relief as soon as Hodges was out of earshot. For the obvious reasons, Jackson had been the target of unrelenting ridicule since he first applied for this program (probably long before that), but he didn't take the humiliation any more personally than the next guy. He understood, like his classmates, that the short guys were going to be made fun of for being too short, the tall guys for being too tall, the fat guys for being too fat, and so on. It was just the nature of the beast, and they would all have to endure it.

Meanwhile, Hodges had already forgotten Jackson and started digging into Richardson.

"Riddle me this, Batman: if you can't even remember to bring your paddle with you when you do a coxswain report, how can we trust you not to forget your rifle when you go out on a mission?"

Stokley, Peterson, and Dunn had slipped over the berm unnoticed a few minutes earlier, waiting for the least pleasant time to present themselves.

"Wait, Chief. I forgot my rifle. Can we turn the chopper around to go get it?"

"Chief, I forgot my bullets. Let's take this submarine

66

back to port and risk losing track of Osama while I run back to the armory and get some!"

Stokley and Peterson continued to taunt Richardson, who was struggling to maintain his cool.

"Richardson," Hodges spoke once again, "how about I go down to your boat and bring you back your paddle? How does that sound?"

"Instructor Hodges, I can go get my paddle." Richardson's tone suggested that he was fighting to hold back either tears or fists.

"Apparently not, Richardson. We already gave you your chance. Now that we know you're a fuck-up, we're all going to have to work harder to carry your share of the weight since you can't handle it." Hodges turned around and walked down the berm, returning a moment later, oar in hand. However, instead of handing it off, Hodges sidestepped around Richardson so that he was positioned directly behind him.

Richardson felt the stock of his oar hit him squarely in the back, padded sufficiently by his life vest not to cause serious damage, yet forcefully enough to send him tumbling down the berm. Hodges threw the paddle down after him.

"There's your fucking paddle! Boat-crew Twenty-Five, hit the surf. When you get back, everybody but Richardson, drop down." He stepped through the gap he had created in the formation of coxswains.

"Does anybody else want to report without his paddle?"

"Negative, Instructor Hodges!" sounded the remaining thirty coxswains.

"I didn't think so." Hodges removed his sunglasses to reveal a set of eyes so faintly blue they looked gray in the light haze of the morning. He might have been the only instructor ever to work at BUD/S who was more intimidating without his shades on. Now there was nothing to shield the assembled coxswains from the cold, hard gaze of those horrible, merciless, ravishing blue eyes.

"Who here can tell me what makes the difference between an amateur and a professional?" Hodges waited for a response, but nobody raised a hand.

"The difference is that an amateur never gives up until he succeeds. An amateur works hard and applies himself efficiently. If he has to, an amateur will practice a skill over and over again until he gets it right. A professional practices that same skill until he never gets it wrong."

As Hodges strolled up and down the line, he made it a point to establish eye contact with every single coxswain he passed.

"I bet Richardson is a pretty squared-away guy. I bet you all are. That's how you made it to BUD/S. But nobody cares about how much shit you've done correctly up until this point. All I look for in you is what you do wrong, what is going to compromise you and your buddy when you're out in the Teams, when the heat is on and lives are at stake, and when I look, I see everything."

Hodges put his glasses back on and continued inspecting trainees where he had left off, sending each one back down the berm to join his boat-crew after reporting.

By now, Peterson and Stokley had started weaving in and out of the boat-crews still awaiting their coxswains at the water's edge, the rising tide beginning to reach the boots of those trainees in the 'one' position.

Peterson went to the south end of the formation, towards those boat-crews whose coxswains had already reported.

"If your boat-crew leader has already reported in, go get wet!" he yelled.

"If your boat-crew leader has already reported, get wet!" echoed the class.

A few dozen trainees began running towards the surf, none forgetting to take his oar with him. Scattered 'Hoo-yahs' were heard coming from them as they dropped into the water just deeply enough to completely inundate themselves and sprang back up to return to the beach.

Drake, still awaiting Phelps' return, tried to enjoy the last few moments of dryness he'd have today. He thought back to the introduction to surf passage class they had been given during week two of indoctrination.

'After lining yourselves up on the beach, facing the water, whichever instructor is leading the evolution will call a coxswain report. At that time, all boat-crew leaders will line up atop the berm, facing the water, and all other boat-crew members will stand at attention in their respective boat-crew positions. Coxswains will be briefed on proper procedure for reporting before hand, but you should all get to know these procedures just as well as your boat-crew leaders do, since most of them are going to be replaced by one of you sooner or later. Once every coxswain has reported and returned to his respective boat-crew, the class will be issued a set of instructions to carry out. These will involve some combination of paddling your IBS out past the surf zone, 'dumping boat' to get all the water out of it you're sure to have collected, and returning to shore to dump boat at the waterline and perform a series of up-boat/down-boat drills.'

§

Within minutes, every trainee stood at attention with his boat-crew, soaking wet. Instructor Hodges now stood with Peterson and Stokley, a few yards behind Boat-crew Fifteen.

"Class 269, when I say, you are to paddle out past the surf zone, dump boat, paddle north to the yellow beach marker, paddle in to shore, and run your boats around the berm back into formation where you stand now!"

"Dump boat and paddle to the yellow beach marker!" shouted Kuslidge to clear up any misunderstandings.

"Dump boat and paddle to the yellow beach marker!" replied the class.

"Bust 'em!" came Hodges' voice from the megaphone.

"Prepare to low carry. Low carry!" instructed Phelps. He and all six other members instantly grabbed their respective handles to lift the IBS and took off running into the surf, now the biggest it had been since they arrived at the formation. To some, this would have seemed like bad luck, to others karma, but those trainees who knew better were well aware of a BUD/S Instructor's mystical ability to manipulate the waters at will in order to make conditions the least pleasant for his trainees.

In moments, Drake and Driscoll were in knee-deep, still plowing forward at full speed, despite the drag of their BDU pants, showing no regard for the temperature of the water, which must have been around fifty degrees Fahrenheit.

"Ones in!" Phelps shouted from the rear of the boat.

"Ones in!" repeated Drake and Driscoll as they mounted the outer tubing of their IBS, one leg inside, the other hanging out of the boat, boots just above the surface of the water.

"Twos in!"

"Twos in!"

And finally, "Threes in!"

"Threes in!" Phelps, almost waist-deep now, gave their IBS a hard shove forward before jumping in himself and beginning to call stroking cadence.

"Stroke... stroke... stroke..." all members of Boat-crew Two chanted in unison. From both sides, they could hear other boat-crews calling their own cadences, or singing, or trying to decide how far out to paddle before dumping boat.

Boat-crew Two was a little ways ahead of the pack, Boat-crews One and Five not far behind. About ten yards ahead, a wave had formed and was heading straight towards them. It couldn't have been any higher than three or four feet.

"Wave coming, get ready to lean into it!" shouted Driscoll from the front of the boat.

"Right side, stroke harder. Straighten us out!" ordered Phelps, doing what he could to steer them from the rear, using his oar as a rudder.

"But, Honey, I'm stroking as hard as I can!" whined Brown in the most feminine tone he could produce. Nobody slowed his cadence as they chuckled briefly.

"Now, lean!" All seven members of the boat crew leaned forward together as the front end of their boat climbed over the crest of the wave, and then dived down into the water beyond it, shaking Gilbert off balance and sending him right into Seaman Hernandez' back.

"Watch where you're going, dumbass!"

Gilbert tried to work out something of an apology but his life vest was caught in his mouth. All he managed to do was blow water and snot out of his nose onto Hernandez' neck. Hernandez didn't seem to notice, so Gilbert didn't tell him.

Drake looked off to his left to the spot where Boat-crew Five had been, and still was, just not in their boat anymore. It was far too early to dump, he thought. 'They must have hit that wave sideways and been flipped by it. Too bad for them!' He faced forward again and kept stroking, being careful to keep pace with the rest of his crewmates.

"Got another wave building up ahead. This one looks bigger."

"Pick up the pace. If we're lucky, we might get over it before it crests." Phelps began calling their cadence faster, and paddling himself.

The swell was growing rapidly as it drove towards them. It would be close to six feet tall before it crested. Two was no longer racing against the other boat-crews. Right now, they were racing against the surf and they were losing.

"Stroke... stroke..." They were still fifteen yards from the wave, and it was building higher and higher, little bits of white water now visible at the top.

"It's cresting!"

"Lean forward! Keep stroking into it!" Drake gasped as a great deal of water crashed into him, the nose of their IBS barely clearing the top of the wave. He was now soaking wet all over again, with fresh, cold ocean water. He felt the cold shock his breath away and took a few quick breaths to calm himself down. He was getting more used to the sensation, but had decided weeks ago that he would never learn to enjoy it.

Their IBS bent slightly as it passed over the wave.

As flat as it was, Drake was surprised it hadn't folded in half. They were now sideways in the water, facing north, each trainee still trying to regain his bearing.

"Grab your buddy! Grab your buddy!" Phelps yelled at full volume.

Drake pulled his paddle in close to his body, clutching it tightly with his left hand as he reached through Driscoll's life vest with his right, just in time.

Another wave, as monumental as the last if not more so, crested over the entire IBS, engulfing it. Drake sucked in as much air as he could before the boat flipped and rolled, turning side over side. He was thrown out with far more force than he'd anticipated. He felt his arm come free of Driscoll's vest as they both tumbled under the water in different directions.

Drake didn't do anything to fight back, just held his breath in as tightly as he could. He felt something hit him in the gut hard. 'Probably one of the other trainee's heads,' he figured.

Moments later, Drake finally came to a stop, still not knowing which way was up. His vest brought him to the surface in a matter of seconds.

He looked around, finding first the beach, then an overturned IBS, a few trainees scattered around it. He identified them as being from another boat-crew entirely. At least he still had his paddle.

"Boat-crew Two!" Drake heard Phelps' voice coming from behind him, from the south it must be, since the beach was to his right, and turned to see his own IBS floating upside down twenty yards away.

He swam to it water polo style, keeping his head above the water to maintain situational awareness, collecting two stray paddles on the way. He was the fourth man from his boat-crew to return. Driscoll, Phelps, and Gilbert were already there, floating in the water waiting. Drake began to notice again how cold the water was as his senses steadily returned to him. Without meaning to, he was pulling his knees upward into his chest, instinctively lessening his posture to insulate his core.

"That's a good enough dump for me, even if it was by accident. Let's get this thing flipped back over and pick up the rest of the guys before we head north."

Gilbert climbed onto the inverted craft and grabbed the middle port-side handle. He stood up and leaned back with it as Phelps, Driscoll, and Drake pushed upward from under the main port side inflation tubing to roll the craft back over. By now, Hernandez had also found his way back.

The five of them jumped in together and began sounding off for Brown and Branson.

"Boat-crew Two!"

"Boat-crew Two!" returned Branson from a little ways north.

They spotted the two stragglers floating in each other's arms and began to paddle towards them, keeping an eye out for any large waves that might be heading their direction.

"You two make a cute couple."

"Shut up and get us into the boat! I'm freezing!"

Driscoll extended an arm and helped Brown and Branson aboard.

"Everyone got a paddle?" asked Phelps.

Five trainees nodded their heads.

"Nope, I'm missing one," said Hernandez.

Drake handed him one of the extras he had acquired.

"I've still got one extra."

"Looks like someone in Boat-crew Four is shit out of luck." Phelps pointed to the disoriented boat-crew searching desperately for their missing oar east of where Boat-crew Two sat. "We can work it out when we get back to shore. We're pretty much past the surf zone. It's just swells this far out. Keep paddling north until we cross the yellow marker. On the way, be checking yourselves over to make sure your blouses and covers and whatnot are stilled configured properly." Phelps put his own oar back in the water and started paddling with his boat-crew, softly calling cadence.

"Oh! There goes another one!" Instructors Dunn and Stokley roared with laugher as Boat-crew Eleven was crushed by a wave. Four of its members, including the coxswain, were thrown out of the boat, which, having failed to rollover when the wave hit, was now full of water. The remaining three boat-crew members jumped out after their buddies and tried to dump their IBS without luck.

"Nope, they're not going anywhere."

"Now that Eleven's out, who's your money on, Hodges?" asked Stokley.

"I'm sticking with Two. One may have taller dudes, but they don't even come close to matching the power those guys are putting out."

"No shit. I bet the dynamic duo sitting in the Ones' spots could carry that boat all by themselves if they had to," said Peterson.

"Hold that thought. It gives me an idea for our next log PT." Dunn smiled smugly as he wrote a note in the green binder that always accompanied the sunglasses and spittoon cup.

§

Driscoll looked around in the direction of the beach, trying to determine the positions of the other boat-crews. He spotted Boat-crew One ahead of them, alongside Boat-crew Eight. He didn't bother to see who might be coming up from the rear. Driscoll's goal for this evolution was to beat out the lead boat-crew and finish first. "It pays to be a winner," the instructors always told them. It wasn't uncommon for the winner(s) of a given evolution to be rewarded in the form of extra rest during the evolution, or early dismissal.

They had also said that the easiest way to keep warm during water evolutions was to put out at one-hundred percent, and Driscoll had begun shivering since having been thrown out of the boat. The increased effort level would help elevate their core temperature enough to slow the onset of hypothermia.

"Driscoll, how's that knee doing?" Drake asked.

"It's the least of my worries right now. This water's so fucking cold, especially at six percent body-fat. I just don't have enough insulation." Driscoll looked down at his stomach, as if he expected to be able to tell through the utility blouse whether or not his abs were still on par with a professional fitness model's.

"Stop your whining. We're all cold, even those of us who aren't six percent body fat," said Branson from behind Driscoll.

"Focus, guys. We just passed the beach marker. Start turning us towards the beach," Phelps said as he switched his paddle back into rudder mode.

The surf wasn't quite full strength anymore, but they would still need to be careful to avoid getting tossed again.

"Boat-crews One and Eight are barely ahead of us. If we catch one of these swells right, we can ride it all the way in and take the lead."

"You're right. Keep stroking in steadily. We're a little too far out to get any good distance out of these swells."

They were about a hundred and twenty yards out from the beach, slowly gaining on Boat-crew Eight. Straight ahead of them was the yellow beach marker. They would need to run their IBS north around it and cross the berm before heading south to where the instructor staff was waiting. They could then pass back over to the beach side of the berm and fall into formation.

"There's a swell about the right size starting to form up behind us," Phelps said, glancing over his shoulder, "Pick up the pace a little and we might be able to catch it."

Phelps used his oar to keep their IBS as perpendicular to the approaching wave as possible, while the other members of the boat-crew chanted cadence, steadily increasing the tempo.

"Here it comes. Everyone lean back and keep paddling forward fast!"

The swell was just starting to crest as it caught the tail end of the boat, hoisting Boat-crew Two smoothly, but forcefully upward. Drake felt himself jerk upward for an instant and then came the same pushing-back-into-the-seat sensation of forward acceleration created by his Porsche. Their timing had been perfect.

"Hoo-yah!" yelled Branson and Gilbert as they continued surfing atop their wave, rapidly approaching Boat-crew One.

In a moment, they were ahead of Boat-crew Eight, who had failed to catch the wave and ride in with them. They were headed right for Boat-crew One's tail.

"It looks like we're gonna hit 'em!"

"Don't stop paddling now. If we collide, it'll be their problem, not ours."

Boat-crew Two stroked harder and harder, gaining speed to keep up with the wave as it crested underneath them.

"Look out!" Phelps was yelling to Greenwood and the other members of his boat-crew who seemed oblivious to the IBS about to ram them at full speed.

"Everybody duck! Paddles in!" shouted Greenwood to his crewmates.

All but one of them managed to assume a protected position as the approaching wave sent Boat-crew Two sailing right overhead. The port side of IBS-Two slid overtop the starboard side and three starboard trainees of Boat-crew One.

Muffled yells came from several of Boat-crew One's members. The protests of those who weren't underneath Boat-crew Two were drowned out by the water rushing around them.

Seaman Hernandez felt the end of his paddle thump against the back of Quartermaster Third-Class Vincent's head. "Sorry!" he called out somewhat insincerely as he and Gilbert laughed with unsympathetic amusement.

"He's definitely going to be feeling that one tomorrow."

Boat-crew Two surfed in until they were floating in only two feet of water.

"Ones out."

"Ones out!" Drake and Driscoll replied as they

jumped down into the water and began dragging the boat into shore.

"Twos out."

"Twos out!"

"Threes out." Phelps, Gilbert, and Brown hopped out together and helped their crewmates push their IBS up onto the beach.

"Dump boat!" shouted Phelps as he and his crew turned their boat sideways and tipped it towards the berm. Each man made sure not to position himself between the small craft and the beach. No less than fifteen gallons of water poured out into the sand.

"Prepare to up boat. Up boat!" Boat-crew Two brought the IBS to rest atop their heads once more and started running towards the berm, going at full speed in spite of their being at least twenty yards ahead of Boat-crew One, the closest to them.

They were trying their hardest to traverse smoothly over the sandy surface of the beach, but neither their best efforts at grace nor their comparable heights were enough to keep the IBS from bouncing violently with every step. Drake did what he could to ignore the pounding on his neck and the chafing on the sun-burnt skin of his head as his pushed his handle forward and leaned the weight of his body with it to pull the trainees struggling behind him.

"Handles forward!" he and Driscoll yelled in unison.

In thirty seconds they were over the berm. In three minutes, they had ventured far enough south and crossed back over the berm, returning to the beach-side and taking their place in the southernmost position of the original formation. The other boat-crews were still quite a ways behind, some still not even back to shore.

"One, two, three," counted Phelps softly.

"Hoo-yah, Boat-crew Two!" they all hollered as they came to a halt.

Hodges broke away from the instructor cluster and came over to meet them.

"Yeah, Hoo-yah," he muttered sarcastically, "Why don't you guys sit down and take a breather?"

"Hoo-yah, Instructor Hodges."

"Prepare to down boat. Down boat," Phelps said. Boat-crew Two lowered their IBS gently into the sand, out of reach of the waterline, and took seats on the primary inflation tube, by now so flat that they sank into it like a beanbag chair.

"Rest up while you have the chance. We'd hate to see you too gassed to put out this afternoon." Hodges eyed Drake slyly as he turned and departed.

5

Senior Chief Grand was seated at his desk. He looked around at the walls of the tiny office, cluttered with pictures and souvenirs from a long and exciting, but strangely unfulfilling career. Among them he saw a black and white photograph of himself shaking hands with Robert Cummings, BUD/S class 244's 'honor man,' at their graduation ceremony. Now, only four and a half years later, Cummings was stationed at Naval Amphibious Base Little Creek in Virginia Beach, Virginia, and had just been frocked to Special Warfare Operator First Class. Under normal circumstances, it wouldn't have been possible to advance so quickly, but Cummings had been meritoriously promoted for displaying exceptional leadership potential, military bearing, and above all, aptitude for killing rag-heads in third world shitholes.

The image brought to mind a hopeful, but unrealistic thought. 'What if every SEAL could be like that? What if we didn't constantly have to deal with problem cases like Stokley, devoting gratuitous amounts of time and energy to salvaging the careers of guys who would always be just another dirt bag who slipped through the system and got his Trident? Ah, Stokley, how good it will be to leave your memory behind when I retire in six weeks. My days of giving you undeserved second chances are finally at an end.'

Despite having accrued a relatively lengthy list of achievements himself, Grand still hadn't made Master Chief and didn't think he was likely to anytime soon, so he had made the decision to retire at the end of his current enlistment, which would come about the time Class 269 was scheduled to finish first phase. He hadn't announced it officially yet, but most of his staff and co-workers could already see it coming.

He examined the next item atop the mound of paper-work that lay before him. It was the approval for Hodges' early discharge request chit. Hodges had submitted it a while ago, admittedly (to Grand alone) with the intention of signing a contract with TCC International, although his official reason had been a 'desire to return to college and further his education.'

But he always had been after the money. From Hodges' point of view, there was probably no point in staying in the Navy when he could sign on with any of the major private military contracting corporations currently employed by the U.S. government and bank triple or quadruple what he was being paid now.

23JUL2007: BUD/S Compound First Phase Office, Coronado, CA.
"I don't like the idea any more than you do, Senior, but we've both got the rest of our lives to get on with and neither one of us wants Stokley to be hanging around in our closet for it, waiting to let slip the wrong hint during the wrong session of belligerency."

"I understand your reasoning and I agree that it would be best to get him out of the picture sooner rather than later, but here at BUD/S? This is the most closely scrutinized, most closely monitored training command in existence. How do you know this guy can pull it off?"

"He's had overwhelming success with every other challenge he's ever faced, whether it be academic, athletic, legal, you name it. Why should he be any less brilliant when it comes to assassination?"

"Even if he's as capable, or as lucky, as you say, what makes you so sure he'll follow through? I know plenty of really tough guys who wouldn't make it one day at BUD/S, and your man would have to do several weeks of it, on top of four to six months of boot camp and BUD/S Prep."

"It's not going to be cheap, but you know Master Chief is going to take leave to go see his family the last weekend in January, like he always does, and that'll make you the senior enlisted leader of the compound, temporarily giving you the authority to make a withdrawal from the emergency fund."

"Yes it does, but what are we supposed to tell the Commanding Officer when the rest of the command finds that they're missing, exactly how much?"

"Five hundred thousand dollars, but they won't know that because by the time they figure out you've trashed the record of how much belongs in that cash reservoir, you'll be long gone. It wouldn't be the first time that particular scenario has happened here, would it?"

"Remember who you're talking to, Hodges. Scheming co-conspirator or not, I'm still your superior for the next nine months."

"You're three pay grades my senior, but you're not my superior."

By now, Boat-crew Two had long since rejoined their class in the regular 'course of instruction.'

"Up boat!" yelled Stokley through Dunn's

megaphone.

"Up boat!" yelled the class as they heaved their IBSs overhead, maybe for the hundredth time today, maybe for the thousandth.

"Down boat!"

"Down boat!"

"Up boat!"

"Up boat!"

"Extended arm!" Every boat rose off the heads of its crew members. Trainees all around strained to keep their elbows locked as bitch faces began emerging left and right.

Instructor Peterson walked up to Practicing Paul, who seemed to be struggling more than most. It wasn't necessarily a sign that he was weaker, maybe just that he was trying harder, or failing to conceal his pain as well.

"Seaman Paul, are you hurting?"

"Hoo-yah, Instructor Peterson."

"I've got news for you, Paul. Life is going to hurt. Life as a SEAL hurts. It doesn't getting any easier when you finish Hellweek, when you finish BUD/S, or when you finish SQT and get pinned. Life never gets easier. You get harder."

Peterson knelt down on the beach and dipped his fingers into it, emerging with a fistful of sand as he addressed Paul once more. "Seaman Paul, right now and every day for the rest of your life, you're going to have to make the choice between that," Peterson pointed to the west, at a Navy cruiser sailing out of 32nd Street Naval Station, undoubtedly crewed by at least one recent BUD/s dropout, "and this." He opened his fist in front of Paul's face, letting the sand pour out and return to the beach.

"Hoo-yah, Instructor Peterson."

At the same time, several boat-crews away, Instructor Dunn was having a chat with Seaman Withers, who also appeared to be struggling.

"Seaman Withers, you're making that boat look awfully heavy. Are you about to quit on us?"

'Stay cool and he'll go away.' "Negative, Instructor Dunn."

"I don't know if I believe you, Withers."

'Shut up, asshole. What do you know?'

"Everyone in your boat-crew but you has his arms locked out, Withers."

'Lock 'em out. Just ten seconds and he'll go away.'

"So, you're strong enough to lock your arms out when I'm watching you, but what about when I stop holding your hand and go check on the next weak piece of shit?"

'Ignore him. It's almost over, has to be.'

"You know what, Withers? I think I may just make you my little project. If what you need in order to keep putting out is for me to follow you around and spoon-feed you motivation, that's what I'll do."

'Fuck it. This isn't what I signed up for.' "Seaman Withers, DOR."

"OIC, LPO!" yelled Hodges.

"OIC, LPO!" Vickers and Kuslidge broke away from their boat-crews and sprinted up the berm to meet Instructors Hodges and Stokley.

"Sir, what time does your brief with Master Chief Talbert begin?"

"0930, Instructor Hodges."

"Okay, you now have sixty seconds to get every trainee and every IBS over the berm and off my beach. If you're late, we can all come back and keep doing up-boat drills until somebody breaks a collarbone."

"Hoo-yah, Instructor Hodges."

Both class leaders had begun addressing the class almost before they finished Hoo-yahing Hodges. Boat-crews were already sprinting every which way, some rushing straight for the barracks and their respective storage racks, others trying to flank the rest of the class and get around them, thinking it would be faster than waiting behind the mob of trainees directly ahead.

Drake's boat-crew was already ahead of the pack, having finished the IBS PT at the south end of the formation, closest to the barracks, and was able to get out of the way quickly. Immediately after helping his crew stow their IBS, he began changing back into his usual uniform.

With a quick pass through the high pressure de-con showers, he dropped off his life vest in his drying cage compartment, then proceeded to the gear formation to exchange covers, re-equip his canteen belt, and place his ID, room key, etc. back into the correct pockets and pouches; but when he got around to the outer north wall of the drying cage, he thought at first a tornado might have blown through while they were out for surf passage.

Drake glanced around desperately for a couple seconds. There was no chance anybody was going to find his way around this mess. There was gear strewn about everywhere.

He heard Kuslidge's voice coming from the direction

of the berm, "Thirty seconds left, move!" and then Vickers' voice from inside the drying cages, "When you finish changing out, head into the classroom and start setting up seats!"

Drake ran back into the drying cages to find Vickers and began explaining what he'd found, "The instructors tossed our gear while we were out on the beach. It's not even close to being in boat-crews anymore, Sir."

Vickers glanced around the corner to see for himself. His jaw dropped, plastering on his face an expression similar to what it might have displayed if he'd caught someone keying his Volvo. He stood petrified, unsure how to respond.

"269, the instructors tossed our grounded gear! Everybody just grab something and go to the classroom. We'll get everything sorted out once we're inside!" yelled Call to the class.

The class began passing the word, everybody grabbing a handful of canteen belts or hard covers, or whatever else was nearest to him.

Drake waited for Driscoll to drop off his life vest and they started jogging south, weaving through those trainees who weren't ready yet, of which there were plenty (although every boat-crew had miraculously managed to meet Hodges' time standard and evacuate the beach).

They approached the classroom and came to a halt at the doorway. Seaman Clarke had posted up at the entrance and was taking a head count of those entering.

"Hey, Clarke," said Driscoll, being concise partly because he didn't want to interrupt Clarke's count, partly because he was still out of breath.

"Seventeen, eighteen. Come on in boys!" Clarke's voice still carried the same joyful, carefree tone it always did. It was a mystery to Drake how optimism could survive in a place like this.

They entered and uncovered, each dropping a pile of 'gear adrift' on the stage at the front of the room before heading to the back and taking seats. 'First evolution of the day down; two more to go.'

6

The members of the class slowly continued to trickle in over the next few minutes, bringing in bundles of stray gear and searching through what had already been deposited in an attempt to find their own. Eventually the room filled up and the stage area emptied of gear adrift.

Drake looked in the direction of the entrance and saw Clarke say something to Kuslidge, probably verifying that the count was correct and all trainees were present. Clarke remained at the entrance, standing watch for any approaching instructors as Kuslidge left him to take his seat by Vickers at the front of the room.

Vickers and Kuslidge talked briefly with each other before Vickers rose to his feet and turned around to face the class.

"Guys, pretty good job so far. We were a little slow getting out there for surf passage, but once we got squared away on the beach, everything went pretty smoothly. I think the only real screw-up we had was Richardson forgetting that paddle. Speaking of losing gear, it looks like we got everything sorted back out after the instructors tossed our staged gear, so Hoo-yah for everyone having their stuff stenciled."

Vickers looked down at his clipboard before speaking again, "One thing we definitely need to be working on more is making sure every IBS is prepped and ready to go the night before any IBS evolutions: surf passage, rock portage, land portage, whatever. Don't get caught off guard like that again. I saw a lot of boat-crews having a really hard time maneuvering out there today because they had flat boats. Boat-crew leaders, you need to be getting with your guys to fix that."

Now it was Kuslidge's turn to put in his two cents. "One other thing we need to be doing is moving with a sense of urgency. Like Chief was saying earlier, it's going to take one hundred percent effort during every single training evolution for us to be successful, and you guys out there who aren't motivated are going to go away, one way or another. If you think it's hard right now, you're going to have another think coming to you when we get to Hellweek. So you -"

"Standby!" yelled Clarke from the doorway.

The entire class arose. For an instant, the room was filled with the screeching of chairs sliding over the tile floor of the classroom, now covered in water and mud, speckled with the boot prints of various sizes of 922s.

"Take seats," said Chief Avilez as he stepped up onto the stage at the front of the room, placing his coffee thermos on the podium.

"Kuslidge, is everyone here?"

"Hoo-yah, Chief."

"Okay, class, Master Chief Talbert is scheduled to come in about fifteen minutes from now, so I'll keep this real short and sweet. I started to see some good shit happening out there during surf passage today. You got off to a rough start being late, but for the most part, teamwork on a boat-crew scale is developing exactly as it should. What needs to happen is for that same kind of coordination to happen across the entire class."

Chief Avilez spoke clearly and his words were well-articulated, more so than the majority of the instructor staff, due somewhat to the fact that he didn't always address them with a pinch of chewing tobacco bulging out of his bottom lip.

"I saw a few boat-crews in particular looking especially motivated. Boat-crew Two, feet."

Boat-crew Two leapt out of their seats and came to attention, with the exception of Brown who was already standing to keep himself from falling asleep.

"These guys were kicking ass out there and it wasn't because they're bigger or stronger, even though they might be, or because their IBS was better prepared, which it obviously wasn't. I'm surprised that damn thing even stayed afloat as flat as it was. It was because Phelps knows what the hell he's talking about, and the rest of his guys worked effectively together as a team when they followed his commands. Boat-crew Two, take seats."

Avilez paced back and forth on the stage as he spoke. It looked as if he were analyzing every trainee he passed, inspecting them for something.

"I can see that you all got your equipment sorted out after the instructors tossed it. You didn't waste time trying to get it all figured out outside. You proceeded to come to the classroom and worked out your issues on the way, saving some time and making sure you didn't get here late. Hoo-yah for hitting that curve ball."

"Hoo-yah!" sounded the class loudly in response.

Avilez pulled a chair out from behind the podium and carried it to the center of the room where everyone was sure to be able to see him and sat down. Any trainees who had been in his way took care to back up, keeping a buffer zone of at least six feet.

"You aren't where you need to be yet, but what you've got now is some momentum. Going back to Boatcrew Two's performance today, part of the reason they beat out One and Eight is because they managed to catch the momentum of the surf and ride it all the way in to victory, when the rest of you just let those waves beat you down over and over instead of using them. Momentum, as you will all hopefully learn in time, is a necessity no matter what the situation. It's a necessity in training every bit as much as it's a necessity in combat. It's not enough just to get off to a good start, or catch up at the end. It is absolutely imperative that everything we do, especially for those of you who actually make it to the Teams, be executed perfectly. Every mistake we make becomes a speed bump, a threat to our momentum, and puts us at greater risk for failure. Right now, you're at BUD/S, but when you get out into the real world, failure will either mean that you or your buddy, or both, are going to get killed."

Avilez looked at his watch before standing and returning his chair to the stage.

"You've got Master Chief Talbert coming in next. I know he likes to get a little relaxed and mushy with you guys, but I still expect everyone here to show proper respect and maintain military bearing when you address him. Am I understood?"

"Hoo-yah, Chief!"

"He should be here any minute, so I'll leave you with that for now."

"Feet!" yelled Kuslidge as Avilez turned and headed for the door. Once again, the class came to attention.

"Okay, take seats," said Vickers once Avilez had exited the classroom. Then he turned to face the class, "It's 0924 now. If you need to make an emergency head call, take a swim buddy and go, but be back in here by 0930."

"Fuuuuuuuuck," sighed Driscoll as he tilted his head back and rolled his eyes, like he always did, "I'm so fucking hungry."

"It must be hard for you to go so long between meals with 'only six percent body fat,'" said Seaman Clarke, who had come over to join Driscoll and Drake, having been relieved as door watch by another trainee.

"Umm, it really is. Back when I was waiting tables at Outback, unless I was taking an order or bringing someone's food out to them, I was back in the kitchen chowing down. I miss those days." He reached into his one of his trouser pockets and removed a packet of galley jelly. He opened it and licked out the entire contents before putting the packet back into his pocket.

"I didn't know the Last Supper was held at Outback," interjected Seaman Branson. Everybody but Driscoll laughed.

"Speaking of food, you guys coming over this weekend?" Clarke asked, "I already know non-practicing Paul is."

"Sounds good to me," answered Driscoll.

"I should be coming. Do you need me to pick anything up on the way?" asked Drake, never failing to remember what he'd been taught at home about being a proper guest.

"If you want you can get some ice cream and milk, since you usually end up cleaning out all we have of both anyway."

"Will do."

Drake settled back into his chair and closed his eyes. It really was a shame he wasn't going to get to finish training with these guys. There was no doubt he'd have been a great match for this program and this bunch of dudes if he'd really intended to go through with it to the end, but he was here for other reasons, and now more than ever it was important that he keep his eye on the target. Even so, his mind began to wander.

27JAN2008: Pine Grove Apartments, Chula Vista, CA.

"Sid, it's good to see you're enjoying my casserole. I had doubts about whether or not it was going to be a hit tonight."

"I think Sid just likes food in general. It takes a lot to fuel those man-guns he's carrying around."

"He's just trying to grow up big and strong like me, isn't that right, son?"

"I think you mean 'grandson,' and Jamie, your cooking really is delicious. I don't know how I survived the last seventeen years without it."

"Sid, I think that's your phone vibrating in the kitchen."

"I better get that. Excuse me."

"Hello...yes...Friday...I'll be there...that's 619-555-2269..."

"You have a hot date or something?"

"You have no idea."

"Urrrggkk!" Hodges vomited again into the toilet in the back of the first phase office. Stokley had just walked in a minute ago and he and Hodges were now the only two in the office.

"That's sounds disgusting. You doin' alright in there?" asked Stokley from the door. He tried to angle his mouth and nose in the opposite direction.

A moment later, he heard the toilet flush inside and stepped away from the door. Hodges opened it and stepped out into the main section of the office.

"I think I ate a bad omelet this morning. You know how that galley can be."

"You ate a bad something. That's for sure. You going to be alright to finish out the day?"

"Yeah, I should be," Hodges said, still wiping the vomit off his face. He didn't have as much practice at vomiting as Stokley, and still occasionally got some on himself. "But could I ask you a favor?"

"Anything, man. What do you need?"

"It'd be really great if you could take the kayak today during the ocean swim. I think I'm just gonna watch that one from the shore."

"Sure, I've got you covered."

"Thanks. Let's go see if we can sneak into Master Chief's presentation. I always like watching those."

7

"Standby!"

Retired Master Chief John Talbert was a large man in his early fifties. He was relatively tall, and retained the same muscular build he'd had since his high school football days, remarkably well preserved for a guy who had spent the greater part of the last three decades running around as a SEAL operator, being shot and stabbed and blown up in the most volatile parts of the world. He appeared now in casual civilian clothes. This would be his third session with class 269 since they started indoctrination.

"No, take seats, everyone. Relax." Hearing a former Navy SEAL speak with such informal tones was still un-settling for the majority of the trainees. Indeed, it would have been more relaxing if he'd told them all to go to Hell.

Talbert strolled into the room as he spoke, position-ing himself directly in front of the stage area, centered between Vickers and Kuslidge.

"How's everyone doing this morning?"

"Hoo-yah!"

"Hoo-yah. I see a lot of guys standing up in the back. I know we may be a little short of chairs and whatnot, but feel free to come up front and sit on the floor, or lay on it if you want, as long as you're not sleeping."

A few trainees came forward and took seats on the floor, but none lay all the way down.

"So, today's Thursday. That means you've just got, what, four evolutions until the weekend?"

"Hoo-yah, Master Chief," said Vickers from his seat at the front of the room.

"Good stuff, and if I'm correct, you're going straight to lunch after I finish with you and then you end the day with a two mile ocean swim. That sounds like an easy day to me."

"Hoo-yah!"

"Today we were scheduled to have a mental toughness brief, but I think instead I'd like to stray a little bit and talk about what I consider to be a related subject: goal setting."

Talbert jumped up onto the stage and collected a marker from the podium before proceeding to the dry-erase board. He was still surprisingly light on his feet for a man who must have been pushing two hundred and twenty pounds or so. Across the top of the board, he wrote the words 'Goal Setting.'

"Before I get started on this presentation, who thinks they can tell me one way goal setting relates to mental toughness?"

Ensign Jones, seated near the front of the class, a couple seats down from Vickers, raised his hand.

"Yes, Mr. Jones."

Jones came to his feet before speaking, "Master

Chief, sometimes when we're in the middle of a tough evolution, instead of trying to look at the evolution as a whole and thinking how hard it's going to be to get through, we can focus on just the next mile, or the next set of push-ups, or just try to make it through the next ten seconds."

"Thank you, Mr. Jones, please sit down. I know the last thing Chief Avilez said to you guys before heading out was probably something about standing up before you speak and rendering proper courtesies, but I think this process will be more productive if we can all relax a little. You're right to listen to the instructors, but as far as seniority is concerned, when you're in this classroom, I outrank everyone in your instructor staff. I report directly to the Commanding Officer, meaning that I'm higher on the chain of command than every other SEAL stationed here, with the exception of the CO himself and the XO, so if I say to relax, it's okay to relax."

Talbert leaned on the podium with his right elbow, his left hand tucked halfway into the pocket of his jeans. He wasn't wearing a belt.

"Mr. Jones is right on track. Here's one of my favorite riddles: 'How do you eat an elephant?'"

"One bite at a time, Master Chief," said a trainee seated on the floor near Kuslidge.

"Exactly. One bite at a time. It's going to be hard to look at BUD/S and try to take it all in at once. For most guys, it's easier to break down the process not only into phases, like the instructors do, but down into weeks, days, evolutions, or even just a single push-up or set of push-ups as Jones was suggesting."

Talbert adjusted his posture somewhat and took a sip from a water bottle he'd brought in with him. Several other trainees around the room proceeded to take sips from their own canteens, following Talbert's example.

"One strategy that I found helpful, especially during Hellweek, was the 'meal-to-meal' plan. How many of you employ this strategy now?"

A few dozen hands rose around the classroom.

"Good, for those of you who haven't heard of it, the meal-to-meal plan is basically a way of making 'bites' out of the evolutions that pass between meals. If whole days are too much for you, try just focusing on getting to lunch, or to dinner, or to breakfast the next morning. During Hellweek, for instance, you know you're going to get fed exactly every six hours, even if it's just an MRE (Meal Ready to Eat) out on the beach, so as long as you can stand one six hour block at a time, you should be able to make it through, right?"

"Hoo-yah." Very few of the trainees scattered throughout the room were put at ease by the thought of any six hour block of Hellweek.

Talbert went back to the dry-erase board and wrote two category titles under the words 'Goal Setting:' 'Short-Term' and 'Long-Term.'

"Now let's discuss a few short-term and long-term goals. Give me some examples of long-term goals."

A few hands went up.

"You there in the back." Talbert pointed to Practicing Paul, seated in the back corner of the classroom.

"Seaman Paul, getting my Trident pinned on and becoming a Navy SEAL, Master Chief."

"Excellent, that's the obvious one. You in front, what do you have?"

"Seaman Alexander, completing Hellweek, Master

Chief Talbert."

"That's also a good goal, and one you'll all have to complete before getting pinned, right?"

"Hoo-yah."

"Let's hear a few short-term goals now. Don't bother raising your hands. Just throw it out if you've got it."

"Preparing my uniform for the inspection on Monday."

"Passing today's ocean swim."

"Passing today's ocean swim with a faster time than whoever just said that."

Talbert raised his hand to silence the class. "It looks like you guys are catching on pretty fast. I've got a proposal for you all," said Talbert as he wrote up on the board a few of the examples he'd heard from the class.

"As a class, let's all come together and make a long-term goal out of each week. For now, let's make the longest plan we've got just making it to each weekend without DORing. I'm scheduled to meet with you again next Friday, so what do you say we make that long-term goal number one?"

"Hoo-yah."

Drake noticed Instructors Hodges and Stokley creep into the classroom through the backdoor. So did a few other trainees but nobody called them out. They didn't want to interrupt Master Chief Talbert's lesson.

"Look who just slithered in the back," said HM3 Gonzales as he pointed to the back of the room. "That guy scares the shit out of me. I swear I could feel those eyes staring right through my soul when he inspected me this morning."

Hodges and Stokley walked to the back of the class and stood in silence, listening just as intently as the trainees around them.

"Now for step two: how are we supposed to go about completing each of our goals? What is going to keep us going from the start to the finish of each goal? What is going to keep us motivated during the countless hours we spend tired and cold and soaking wet?"

A few hands were raised. Talbert went around the class pointing to several trainees to voice their ideas.

"HM3 Phelps, I just try to beat out the rest of the guys around me. I know if I'm doing well enough to stay ahead of the pack, I'm doing well enough to meet the standard required by BUD/S."

"Seaman Driscoll, I like to focus on not just trying to complete an evolution, but putting out the most I can and giving it my all."

"Seaman Apprentice Drake, I remind myself why I'm here and what I'm fighting for," Drake said without emotion, refusing to meet the gazes he'd provoked from Stokley and Hodges.

"You guys aren't 'fighting' yet. Let's not get ahead of ourselves," said Stokley of all people, still standing at the rear of the classroom.

Drake remained silent as he sat back down. He had been at war with Stokley for the last two years, practically frothing at the mouth over the thought of destroying him, even though Stokley didn't know it yet, and wouldn't in time to fight back if everything went according to plan. Everything always did in Drake's world.

"HM3 Gonzales, I think it's best to have a good sense of humor while we train. It can help increase morale and keep us looking on the brighter side of the bullshit – I mean training."

Hodges and Stokley were both clearly annoyed by

Gonzales' remark, but said nothing.

"Those are all good methods, and methods we can use congruously. One other I'd like to discuss is singing. Lieutenant Vickers, what's the status on the class' song book?"

"There is one posted on the outside of every dorm door. We sing cadence as a class on the way to and from most meals, and some boat-crews do it during surf passage and land portage."

"That's good. Singing has been employed for millennia as an indirect means of emotional expression and a method of arousal control." He turned to the whiteboard and added to it the phrase 'Arousal Control,' writing underneath it a paraphrased definition.

"Arousal control is our ability to consciously modify our emotional responses to various stimuli. It's what gives an actor the ability to induce tears on command or a power-lifter the adrenaline rush he needs to push a heavy weight in competition. Without arousal control, we can't succeed in situations that require us to either suppress or enhance an emotion to increase performance levels."

Instructor Hodges spoke up from his post at the rear of the classroom, "Master Chief, mind if I jump in with something?"

"Go ahead, Instructor Hodges." Talbert seemed pleasantly surprised that the instructor presence had something to add to his lesson. It was helpful to the trainees, in Talbert's opinion, to have a variety of genuine SEAL role models during their time in training. Talbert was also glad it was Hodges who spoke up, and not Stokley.

"Master Chief is dead on with this one. An example of good arousal control we saw out on the beach today was Seaman Jackson. Jackson, where are you?"

Seaman Jackson came to his feet, assumed a position of attention, and sounded off, "Hoo-yah, Instructor Hodges." He wasn't significantly taller standing than he was sitting in his chair.

"Hey, Jackson, stand up!" shouted another trainee from across the room. The room filled with laughter from all directions. Even Jackson laughed along as his face went red, not with anger or embarrassment, but with the same amusement as everyone else's.

"That's exactly what I'm talking about," continued Hodges, not laughing but clearly amused, "That short motherfucker has gotten so much shit from everyone since he's been here, but he's never once let it work him up. He controls his emotional arousal by not losing his temper when we make fun of him. Believe it or not, we actually drop a guy from training every couple of classes for lacking good anger-management skills. It's important to know how to keep your cool under any kind of stress, including humiliation," Hodges finished as he returned to the back of the room.

Drake had no problem with arousal control. In boot camp he had put his powerful imagination to work to keep himself awake during the long, monotonous marching practices. He found the easiest way to stay alert in formation was to focus on the one thing of which he wasn't getting any: sex. Marching to the chow hall: sex; marching to the fitness center: sex; marching to the dental clinic: sex. He remembered standing with his division in the drill hall during their graduation ceremony, building in his mind's eye a fleet of porn stars clad in skimpy lingerie to replace the uniformed shipmates standing at attention around him, a blatant hard-on the only violation to otherwise flawless military posture.

"What Mr. Jackson already manages to do on his own, some of us may need a little help with, which is where our verbal methods of arousal control come into play. Singing, or chanting cadence, as I'd already mentioned is one way to help vent out whatever frustration or pain you may be enduring at the moment. Who can tell me another way?"

"HOO-YAH!" yelled AO2 Dwayne as loudly as he could through fluid-filled lungs and chapped-bloody lips.

An involuntary smile consumed Talbert's entire face before he had a chance to respond, "There's the golden phrase. Hoo-yah. What is the dictionary definition of 'Hoo-yah?'"

There was silence throughout the room until Talbert spoke again.

"You're all absolutely right, every single one of you. There isn't one. Hoo-yah can mean whatever you want it to mean. When those instructors tell you to hit the surf, the 'Hoo-yah' you give in response can mean 'go fuck yourself' if you want it to. 'Hoo-yah' is the only weapon you have in your verbal arsenal to fight back against the BUD/S Instructor, so use it. You should all be Hoo-yahing your asses off every day."

The class gave a series of loud, defiant Hoo-yahs, in spite of the instructor presence at the back of the room. 'What were they going to do, beat the class a little harder for it? Probably, but who gives a shit? BUD/S will be BUD/S one way or another.'

"Master Chief, I'm Seaman Apprentice Tucker and I want to talk about my motivation for becoming a Navy SEAL...umm...Master Chief!" Tucker barely managed to get the words out as he stood crookedly at attention in the center of the classroom, head unintentionally cocked to one side.

He had apparently been inspired by the Hoo-yahing of the class, which came abruptly to a halt as soon as he opened his mouth to speak. There was silence throughout the room. Even Talbert seemed to be briefly at a loss for words.

"Well, alright, Seaman Tucker. Go ahead."

Tucker began his rotisserie with Vickers, turning slowly in a circle so as not to leave anyone out. God forbid a single member of the class miss this.

"Hi, everyone...I'm, umm... Seaman Apprentice Tucker and I want to be a Navy SEAL."

There was immediate, reflexive clapping by everyone in the room, but nothing vocalized. Nobody seemed quite sure yet exactly what was going on, except that the stork-like figure of this eighteen-year-old South Dakotan farm boy at the center of their attention was looking a little gawkier than usual today.

"I don't really know where to start so I guess I'll just say that one year ago, I saw the movie Navy SEALs. You know, the one with Charlie Sheen and Ryan Reynolds, and it really got me thinking. Those SEALs, man, they're some tough guys. They really aren't afraid of anything!"

Hodges and Stokley were beginning to shift around uneasily at the back of the classroom.

"My Ma is a really scary woman. She is! I'm not afraid of much, but my mom, man, she'll put the fear of God right into me." As Tucker spoke, his eyes seemed to be getting wider by the word, like he was straining to examine some tiny insect crawling around at the end of the impossibly long nose protruding from his bony facial structure.

Tucker was now facing Talbert as he spoke, "I remember the last thing she said to me before I left for boot camp was 'Jedediah, you come back here without that shiny gold pitchfork on your chest and I'll kill you!' And the last thing I said was 'Yes, Ma'am!'".

"Pitchfork? Hodges, I don't think I'm equipped to handle this. It's turning from an AA meeting into god-damned redneck Oprah. I need to get out of here."

"Go ahead, but I'm going to hang back and see where this goes. I'll see you after lunch."

Stokley headed quickly in the direction of the exit, and very nearly made it. But just as he began pushing open the rear door of the classroom, Tucker caught him, and, failing miserably to maintain the six foot buffer zone between the two of them, glared right into Stokley's eyes.

"Instructor Stokley, I just know that if I can become a SEAL like you and Instructor Hodges and Master Chief, then I'll finally be able to put the fear back into Ma and I'll never be scared of anything ever again."

Stokley stood petrified, an expression of utter disbelief painted across his face. The entire class held its breath in anticipation.

"Back," Stokley paused for a moment before finishing, "Up."

"Hoo-yah, Instructor Stokley," said Tucker softly as he returned to his seat and sat down. He seemed to be the only one in the room not completely dumb-struck by what had just happened.

Instructor Stokley pushed the door the rest of the way open and promptly left, Hodges not far behind him, having changed his mind about staying after all.

Class 269 breathed a soft sigh of relief.

"Kuslidge, what the hell just happened?"

"I don't know, Sir. I'm still trying to figure it out myself."

Vickers jumped out of his seat and turned to face the class, obviously still confused. "Is everyone alright?"

"Hoo-yah," replied the class.

"Hoo-yah," replied Talbert.

"Tucker, I don't want an explanation of whatever that was. Just please don't ever do it again." Vickers returned to his seat. The class shifted its glance back to Talbert, awaiting further comment, or instruction, or anything at all of a sensible nature.

"As you can see, we all have different reasons for being here. I think we'd better save the rest for another day, though. Mr. Vickers, what's next on the class schedule?"

"This is the last scheduled evolution this morning, but Chief Avilez will probably want to come back for some proctor time before we leave for lunch."

"I'll get out of your way then. I hope you all took something from our session today, and I hope to see you all next Friday."

The class rose to attention as Talbert exited the room. The trainee standing door watch signaled Vickers as soon as Talbert was out of earshot.

"Take seats," said Vickers. "Make head calls quickly now if you need to. When you get back, Lieutenant Klein has something to put out regarding EMI."

"Clarke, head call?" asked Drake as he re-equipped his canteen belt and picked up his hard cover.

"Yeah, let's do it."

The pair arose and started jogging towards the men's room just around the corner from the classroom. The opportunity to piss in a toilet instead of down his BDUs was a luxury Drake had learned to appreciate.

8

"No he didn't. Dunn, I know the guy, and it definitely didn't come *all* the way off," said Peterson from across the office as he threw another dart at the life-sized, full-color silhouette poster of Saddam Hussein clutching an AK-47 mounted on his cubicle wall. The dart landed squarely in Hussein's forehead. "Bull's eye."

"Ok, so it didn't come all the way off, but who cares? The guy still shot himself in the dick. He's never going to live that one down." Instructor Dunn tossed a dart as well, at the picture of his ex-wife mounted on the wall of his own cubicle. He missed her figure entirely.

Stokley and Hodges entered the office and moved in the directions of their respective desks.

"Stokley, there you are. You must have heard about that guy in Team Three who shot himself in the dick while deployed in Iraq last year, right?"

"Yeah, who didn't hear about that? Apparently, he was posing for a picture for his girlfriend with his .45 shoved in the front of his pants and it went off by accident."

"It had to happen to someone sooner or later."

"Yeah, I guess, but a Team guy? You know what this means. Long after all of us are retired, after all of us are dead and buried, on will live the story of that dumb shit who shot himself in the dick with his own gun, a story we've got to keep locked up. If this ever gets out, we'll be the laughing stock of the special warfare community. Even the Rangers won't be able to top that one for a while."

"Hey, don't make fun of our Army brethren. They do try so hard."

"Speaking of deployment to Iraq, when are you finally going to leave this place, Hodges? You've been here forever. I don't see how you could stand starting off as an instructor right out of SQT. Didn't you even want to get out and see the world a little first?"

"I'm sure I'll get my chance sooner or later," said Hodges through a clenched jaw, still somewhat insecure about being the only SEAL on the staff not to have seen combat, in spite of having recorded more time as BUD/S staff than any of the other current instructors below the rank of Chief Petty Officer.

"Didn't you guys hear? Hodges here is going to be leaving the Teams altogether in a couple months. He's got an interest in 'furthering his education,' if I remember the wording correctly."

"Yeah, we all know what that means."

"I think it means he's got an interest in getting paid a thousand dollars a day to bodyguard VIPs in the third world."

"Whatever, I'm going to get some chow." Hodges left the office alone and headed for the oldest F-350 sitting on the grinder. It was dark red with a nine-inch lift and still

109

ran well in spite of the obvious wear and tear it had endured over the years, much like Hodges. Team guys like to keep their gear in good working order. The only pieces on it that hadn't been perfectly maintained were the grill and front bumper, still somewhat mangled from the wreck a few years earlier, much like Hodges. He never had gotten around to buying that new Mustang.

Hodges didn't mind being alone, away from the other instructors. As good as he was and always had been at what he did, he would never really fit in with this, or any other crowd.

"Brandt, wake up."

"Huh, what? What?"

"Brandt, you're pissing on my boot. The urinal is that way."

"Oh, right. Thanks," mumbled Seaman Brandt as Practicing Paul took hold of his shoulders and turned him to face the urinal.

Drake rinsed off his hands and face quickly in the sink and then straightened up and started looking around for Clarke. He saw Clarke's boots sticking out from under the stall, toes down.

"Clarke, how's it going in there?" Drake asked as he knocked on the stall door with his fist. The door, apparently unlatched, swung open. Clarke had his head buried half-way in the toilet bowl and there seemed to be some mixture of blood and vomit erupting from him.

"That doesn't look good from here. How long have you been puking blood?"

"Only since Monday when I went to medical about it. They said I should be better in a few days. I guess it's just another symptom of BUD/S-Itis."

Vomiting blood was never a good sign, but it wasn't especially uncommon here. Even Drake hadn't had a sneeze or taken a piss without seeing his own blood in nearly two weeks, and he was holding up better than most of his classmates. The reluctance of trainees to report to sick call for fear of being removed from training prematurely resulted in most everyone having at least a couple of lurking ailments. Candidates usually just accepted the cause of their otherwise inexplicable bleeding/aching/fatigue/etc. as being 'the stress of BUD/S.'

"Let's get you up and get back into the classroom," said Drake as he helped heave Clarke out of the toilet. By now, Brandt and Paul had left, leaving Drake and Clarke as the last swim pair. Clarke took a moment to regain his senses and motioned that he was ready.

"Head clear!" shouted Drake to Kuslidge as he and Clarke entered the classroom. He saw LTJG Klein standing at the front of the class, handsome, fit, confident, and sporting the same cocky, unsympathetic expression he always did.

"Lately, we've been getting some complaints about the assignment of extra military instruction. Apparently, a lot of people are being assigned these duties and they don't seem to know why." Klein paused for a moment to pick a few grains of sand out from his nose.

"Everything we assign is stuff that has to be done anyway. We pick guys to do it if we see you doing something out of line during the work day. It doesn't have to be anything big, really, or dangerous; but if you forget to stencil your T-shirt or if you're late to muster, or whatever, just accept your one day of EMI and don't do it again. It's not a big deal. If anybody still has issues with it, you can come talk to me tonight and the two of us, along with the OIC/LPO will all sit down together and talk about it and pour out our feelings and touch each other until you feel better. Hoo-yah?"

"Hoo-yah."

"Standby!" It was Chief Avilez entering this time.

"Everybody take seats."

"Hoo-yah, Chief Avilez."

"I already got to speak with you all before Master Chief came in, so I think we can skip the proctor time we've got scheduled for now. I just have one question for the class before you head over to chow."

The class waited in anticipation as Avilez peered about and paced back and forth across the stage a few times.

"Who in here was dipping during Master Chief's presentation?" Avilez' tone didn't sound angry, but definitely irritated.

There was silence throughout the class. Many of the trainees were glancing around the room anxiously, waiting for someone to confess and take his punishment, or not and have everyone take his punishment.

Dwayne, seated near the front of the classroom, stood up and came to attention before speaking. "I was dipping during the class, Chief."

"I know you were, Dwayne. I spotted you the moment I walked in here. Just because I don't dip myself, doesn't mean I don't know what it looks like when somebody else is dipping and trying not to look like they are. Bring me whatever you've got on you."

Dwayne walked to the front of the room and handed off two cans of Skoal brand chewing tobacco to Avilez, one wintergreen flavored and one watermelon flavored.

"AO2 Dwayne, you have not one, but two cans on you. Is this just in case you weren't in the mood for one flavor during this evolution you'd have the other handy?"

"Hoo-yah, Chief." Dwayne was clearly in a state of regret, but there was nothing he could do now.

Avilez spoke to the whole class. "By a show of hands, how many of you think it would be fair of me to make Petty Officer Dwayne eat what remains in each of these cans as remediation for dipping during Master Chief's brief?"

Every single trainee, including Dwayne, raised his hand without a second thought.

Avilez let out a loud burst of laughter. "You fucking buddy-fuckers!"

Many trainees began hesitantly, nervously laughing along with him, unsure where this was going.

"That's fucking disgusting! Dwayne, take your seat." Avilez turned around and threw both cans of chew into the trashcan.

"Dwayne, I'm not going to make you eat this dip, but I am going to tell you a story." Avilez pulled a chair off the stage and took a seat at the front of the class.

"When I was in BUD/S, AO2 Dwayne, all those years ago, I occasionally liked to put in a pinch to stay awake during some of our less intense evolutions and, one day during a first phase proctor brief right before a two-mile ocean swim, I happened to get caught by our class proctor, SO1 Thomas.

"Instructor Thomas had been a SEAL nearly eighteen years and still hadn't made Chief. Any opportunity for advancement had been obliterated when he beat up an intelligence officer, a Lieutenant Commander, for calling his dog fat. His dog was fat. It was really fucking fat, but SO1 Thomas just wasn't the kind of guy to whom you say 'Hey, your dog is so fat you could have your trainees use him for log PT.'"

Now slightly more at ease, the class laughed whole-heartedly with Avilez.

"SO1 Thomas didn't waste any time when he caught me with that pinch of Red Man in my bottom lip. He yanked me out of my chair, took what dip I still had left in my pocket, and told me that I was going to start that day's swim with an entire mouthful of Red Man chew and that if I couldn't produce, from my mouth, some significant amount of chew at the end of that swim, I was going to be medically dropped from training for not having a hair on my ass."

Tucker, squirming erratically in his seat, nearly had another outburst in anticipation of hearing how the story finished, but managed somehow to contain himself.

"You better believe I did that whole swim with that chew in my mouth. I stopped twice to throw up and held that chew in my hand while I did and then just put it back in and kept on going. You all better believe I fin-ished with a passing time, too."

Avilez stood up and placed the chair back on the stage where he had gotten it. "You're lucky you were honest with me Dwayne, but I'm not going to let this slide again. The next time I catch somebody dipping during the workday, I'm going to beat your asses until ten guys either DOR or are declared physically incapacitated by my medical staff. Make sure you're back from lunch and lined up on the beach by 1300." The class came to attention as Avilez left the classroom. Nobody doubted his willingness or his authority to deliver on what he had said.

"'69, feet. Everyone, get dressed out and start forming it up in front of the barracks: four ranks to move facing north."

"Four to move north in front of the barracks!"

9

"Are we still a go for this afternoon?" Grand's tone gave away the anxiety even a powerfully masculine voice like his couldn't conceal. This wouldn't be the first time he'd been involved in a shady dealing, but it would be the first time he'd been an active co-conspirator in a Teammate's murder.

"As far as I know, Senior Chief. Did you have any trouble securing the money?"

"No, none at all. I opened up the safe with the combination Master Chief left and made the withdrawal from the emergency fund this morning. By the time anyone notices the money is missing and there's no record of it ever having been withdrawn, we'll both be long gone."

'You're more right than you know, Senior Chief.' Hodges savored the thought.

"How is the drop going to work?" asked Grand.

"Tomorrow morning at 0800, the class will depart for a soft-sand conditioning run down to the demo pits and back. All trainees and instructors should be away from the compound from then until at least 1000 so you'll have the compound to yourself to make the drop."

"Where exactly is the drop location?"

"It'll be in the first phase drying cages, compartment number 024. The target compartment will be the only one without a seabag, until you deliver our seabag containing a half-million. The man I've hired to do the job for us will collect it later that night, when the workday is over and the whole class will be in the cages emptying their lockers of the gear they need to prep for Monday."

"I suppose that during this event, you'll be on the run with 269 and the rest of the instructor staff." Grand's speech was more at ease for the moment. His anxiety was rising and falling unpredictably. He hated not knowing how this was going to turn out, or at least how it was going to turn out for him.

"That's right, Senior."

"This almost sounds too easy. Remind me again what the combination to the drying cage keypad is."

"Two-two-six-nine."

"Runnin' through the Jungle in the Middle of the Day!"

"Runnin' through the Jungle in the Middle of the Day..."

"Big ol' Anaconda Got in my Way!"

"Big ol' Anaconda Got in my Way..."

"I Love Anaconda Hide!"

"I Love Anaconda Hide..."

"Makes me a Condom Just the right Size!"

"Makes me a Condom Just the right Size..."

"269, halt!" Vickers interrupted Branson's cadence to stop the class in front of the dining facility. Those trainees near the back of the formation had to jog a few extra steps to compact the class back to its regular density.

"Halt..."

"Fall out of ranks and start moving into the galley. Use only the west chow line. We need to hurry if we're going to get everyone through in time, so nobody get any cups/drinks. Rinse off your boots with the de-con hose before you go in there!"

"Fall out and use the west line, no cups!" yelled the trainees closest to Vickers. By the time the word had been distorted by several waves of trainee interpretation and passed back to Drake, some were instead yelling 'No spoons!' or 'No plates, stick out your hands!' He knew what they meant.

"This is great. I'm hungry, dehydrated, and going to stay that way because we're rushing through lunch with nothing to drink but what's left in our canteens," complained Branson as he sprinted towards the galley entrance alongside Drake. "At least we only have one more training evolution today." The two used their canteens to rinse off their boots and bypass the gaggle of trainees at the water hose, weighing the prospect of getting to sit down sooner and catch a few minutes of sleep against the risk of even deeper dehydration.

"You assume that the instructors won't want to beat us for a little while after the swim like they did last Tuesday," responded Drake skeptically.

"There's always a little beating after a swim, but that's just to warm us up. I don't think they'd do anything too drastic after the incident we had during yesterday's conditioning run."

The pair made it into the galley ahead of the bulk of the class. Drake grabbed two apples as he passed the fruit bar that shared the same counter as the tableware dispensers. He didn't bother to check the silverware he selected for left-overs missed by the dish washer.

He bit into the first apple and he could feel sand grits crumbling between his teeth as he chewed, in spite of having rinsed his face and hands just half an hour ago. The BDU he was wearing seemed to be ceaseless in its production of sand, but that didn't stop him.

Drake finished both apples by the time he had gotten far enough to order. There was a mildly overweight, middle-aged Hispanic woman working diligently behind the serving counter. He considered attempting to speak Spanish to her, but decided not to stake today's chow on his limited knowledge of the language.

"Ma'am, I'd like a plate of spaghetti and meatballs and a plate with a few chunks of that fish and all the mashed potatoes you can fit with it." The woman quickly slopped everything he'd ordered onto two plates and handed them to him. She didn't say anything, just smiled and winked at him.

"Thank you, Ma'am," he said as he accepted both plates without acknowledging the wink and placed them hastily on his tray. He continued down the line, collecting as much of this and that as his tray would hold: two rolls, four packets each of peanut butter, strawberry jam, and margarine, two whole limes, and three pieces of chocolate cake with thick chocolate frosting.

Back at home, his diet had consisted of little more than lean meats and vegetables, but here, 'runnin' through the jungle,' Drake had implemented a policy of survival eating. His primary dietary objective was to down as many calories as possible before the class left the galley, in the hope that he'd have enough energy to make it through what evolutions stood between him and the next meal. Even eating like he had been, Drake had lost considerable weight since starting BUD/S one month earlier.

Drake headed for the northwestern-most table in their section of the galley. Driscoll, with whom he shared a boat-crew and was required to sit, said he needed that particular table because it gave him the best view of the galley, and it would, of course, be unconscionable to require Driscoll to eat without a view.

As Drake sat down, he immediately began shoveling the contents of his tray into his mouth in no particular order. He held his face just far enough from the plate to remain relatively vigilant of his surroundings.

"They're all out of chocolate cake again! I can't afford to be getting any fewer calories than I already am. Not with-"

"With your six percent body fat?" Drake handed Driscoll a piece of the cake he had scarfed up a minute ago. "I've got you covered." It would be worth the piece of cake to put an end to Driscoll's whining for a few moments.

"I was going to say 'high metabolism.'" Driscoll sat down and joined Drake in devouring an equally enormous lunch.

The two continued to eat in silence. There wasn't any time to talk right now, not for '69's big boys.

Nearby, a few dozen candidates from SWCC class 059-2 were taking seats as well. Drake recognized one of them, Jack Warr, as being from his boot camp division. He had heard these guys were going to be out here at the same time, but hadn't actually seen any of them yet. Warr was wearing a brown T-shirt and the cover tucked into the waistband of his trousers displayed the insignia of a Petty Officer Third Class. 'He must already be starting CQT, the lucky bastard. Oh well,' Drake thought. 'There'll be time to catch up later.'

08JAN2008: BUD/S Compound Supply Depot, Coronado, CA.
  "What size are those?"
  "The top is a large-regular. The pants are regular-long. The covers are both larges."
  "Give me one of the covers and pass the rest back to Drake. I think he said he was short a set."
  "Lock it up! The next item you should have in your seabag is the dive knife! If you do not have a dive knife, sound off."
  "Ensign Jones: dive knife."
  "Seaman Richardson: dive knife."
  "HM3 Phelps: dive knife."
  "Seaman Apprentice Drake: dive knife."
  "Seaman Lombard: dive knife."
  "Damn, Drake doesn't have anything does he? He's already had to ask for a knife, a set of cammies, and a canteen belt set."
  "My knife looks a little dull. I bet we could just sound off and get a couple brand new ones. Nobody ever checks to see who takes what gear anyway."
  "Seaman Hernandez: dive knife."
  "Seaman Gilbert: dive knife."
  "Gilbert, leave that box alone! That's SQT gear."
  "Calm down. I was just looking."

"Clear!"
Vickers turned around to administer the next set of commands to the class as he continued jogging, backwards now, by Kuslidge's side, "As soon as we get to the drying cages, ground gear in boat-crew formation, One to the west, and start changing out for the-" Vickers tripped

on a shred of tire and fell ass first into the powdery sand behind him, stirring up a small cloud of dust.

"When we get to the cages, ground gear in boat-crews, One to the west, and start changing out for the fall!" yelled Phelps from somewhere near the front of the formation as Vickers struggled to get back on his feet before the class trampled over him. The class roared with laughter.

"I meant for the swim!"

"Ground gear and change out..." echoed a few scattered trainees through the rest who were still too busy laughing at Vickers' expense.

Drake was the first trainee from either Boat-crew One or Two to reach the cages, and laid down his hard cover on the pavement outside the west end of the north wall to mark the head of the formation.

By the time the next man from Two caught up with him, Drake was dressed down to nothing but his stenciled white undershirt and black, BUD/S-issue bikini briefs. Neither was substantial enough to provide much warmth. The undershirt, though cotton, was still damp from Surf Passage, and the briefs, whose size had been the topic of much debate since their issue, barely covered enough to be worn legally in public.

He neatly folded the gear he had just removed and headed into the drying cages, which Kuslidge had opened for the class. As far as Kuslidge knew, he, Vickers, Call, and Dwayne were the only trainees who knew the combination to the keypad lock.

Drake reached his compartment, directly above Seaman De la Cruz' and adjacent to Dwayne's. Along the upper edge of the frame was a strip of white athletic tape labeled '024 − SA Drake.' The only contents of the two foot by two foot by three foot tall compartment were Drake's life vest and seabag, both also stenciled with his name.

He ignored the life vest and proceeded to open the seabag. The gear inside was already staged for today's swim, loaded in the reverse order in which it would be equipped. There wouldn't be a grain of sand to be found anywhere inside. Even the sticky rubber material of the fins and dive mask had been meticulously picked clean of the smallest grits.

Piece number one was a standard pair of beige UDT shorts. He slid them quickly up his muscular legs and began to tuck in his shirt before tightening them around his waist. They were just loose enough not to completely cut off circulation through the clearly defined femoral artery and tributary veins branching out into the perfectly proportioned vastus medialis heads of each quadriceps.

As Drake began reaching back into the bag for the next item, he saw Phelps run past him, wearing only his briefs and T-shirt. Phelps had apparently mixed-and-matched some of his buddies' stencils and written over the seat of his trunks the words 'BUDS STUD.'

"Phelps, really? 'BUD/S stud?' These little panty-things are gay enough without your sense of humor," protested a nearby trainee, eyeing Phelps critically.

"It was your mother's idea," Phelps said as he ventured deeper and deeper into the cages.

"'BUD/S dud' would probably be a better fit."

Phelps pretended not to hear him as he continued to get dressed. Come Hellweek, everyone would know who was going to make it and who wasn't.

"What's up, Drake?" asked Seaman De la Cruz in heavily accented English.

"Nada más que nunca. Podemos hablar en español si prefieres," replied Drake in passable Spanish. Most of the members of the class were developing a working knowledge of the language, living so close the border, but what very few of them knew about Drake was that he also spoke French and German fluently. Drake's father had insisted from an early age that there was no substitute for the ability to communicate effectively, except, when no other option remained, the ability to annihilate effectively, as Drake felt was the case with Stokley.

"Gracias por la oferta, pero creo que me falta la práctica en inglés."

"Fair enough, let me know if you change your mind."

Drake had donned most of his swim apparel: UDT shorts, wetsuit, inflatable UDT vest, carbon dioxide canister for use with said vest, dive booties and dive hood. He pulled his fins out of the seabag and slid his left hand through the heel straps of both so that they hung comfortably on his left wrist. The metal adjustment clips on the heel straps of the fins had been taped over with black electrical tape to prevent them from shining. This was to keep them from being spotted by the Al Qaeda according to MA2 Corbin. Drake suspected that the concentration of Al Qaeda operators in Coronado would be relatively low this time of year, at least compared to the concentration of sharks, but kept his opinions to himself.

He performed a quick self-check, fingering each piece of gear to make sure it was where and how it needed to be. The one piece that never seemed to please his perfectionist attitude was the wetsuit. It was a black, lycra bodysuit, the sleeves full-length, but the legs stopping at about mid-thigh. Scattered over the better part of the upper torso and sleeves were many tiny, little tears and holes, the kind of which one would take for granted during gear-issue, but never again once he felt the chilly ocean water flow in and out with every stroke. Drake figured there were probably two or three of these breaches for every one of about a dozen names to have been stenciled down the spine in white fabric ink and later crossed out by the next owner.

At last, he pulled the final item from the seabag: the dive knife. It was brand new, the blade still coated with the flat black anti-rust finish, and still perfectly sharp — sharp enough to shave the hair on his arm. This would be Drake's first time to take it out with him, having used the older, already tarnished dive knife he was originally issued for previous swims. That knife was now stashed in the trunk of the Porsche.

26JAN2008: Peak Physique Fitness Center, Naval Amphibious Base, Coronado, CA.
"Stokley will be in a kayak waiting at the turnaround when you approach it. He'll be requiring every swim-pair to take a soil sample from the bottom before heading back towards the starting line, giving you a window of about twenty-five seconds to break away from your swim buddy and make your move."
"That's longer than I need."
"It is if you don't hesitate."
"I've been waiting two years for this. I'm not about to fuck it up in the last twenty-five seconds."
"The kayak itself is buoyant enough that it should roll right over as you tip it. Stokley will be disoriented as he goes under. Even so, he's still a SEAL and a combat veteran. If you don't hit your mark on your first try, you may not get another."
"I can handle my side of the deal. Just phone me with the combination to the keypad lock and make sure Grand is in position with the money."

§

Drake removed the canteen from the left side of his web belt and replaced it with the dive knife before wrapping it around his waist. He then grounded all of his dry gear outside with his hard cover and, with De la Cruz at his side, started jogging towards the beach to get lined up for the pre-swim equipment inspection.

As he reached the bottom of the berm, he could feel the consistency of the ground beneath him change from the solidity of the concrete surrounding the drying cages and CBH to powdery soft sands. The grains shifted out from underneath his dive booties as each step landed, providing a much more comfortable reception for his stride and reducing somewhat the pounding sensation in his aching knees.

Drake had developed an absolute loathing for these swims. Hanging out in fifty degree water for over an hour was not at all his idea of a good time, not even in a wetsuit, but today's swim was different. The anticipation he felt now was the same pre-game anxiety he had felt a thousand times before, in the final moments preceding every one of countless other victories. He felt it now stronger than ever.

Drake and De la Cruz made their way over the berm and took their places just north of HM2 Dear and Seaman Cooke, just south of Driscoll and Dwayne. De la Cruz, the senior man, faced the water while Drake faced the berm.

They stood up their fins to their north sides. Inside the foot of one fin, most trainees liked to leave a glob of silicone jelly to spread over the blades of their dive knives after inspections to prevent the integrity of the blade from deteriorating throughout the swim. Drake didn't bother today. This would be the only time he used that particular dive knife.

Up the leg of his wetsuit, Drake had tucked the CO_2 canister for ease of carrying since it wasn't to be inserted into the vest until after it had been inspected by an instructor. This was also a common practice among trainees. One trainee in particular, AO3 Ackerman even liked to urinate down the leg of his wetsuit all over his CO_2 canister before handing it off to whichever instructor was unlucky enough to inspect him that day.

That was just his way of saying 'Fuck you, BUD/S.'

It was gently overcast this afternoon, the sun just managing to peek through the clouds here and there, but relatively warm, maybe seventy-five degrees or so. Drake was beginning to sweat in his wetsuit, but that didn't bother him. Drake had made himself a promise weeks ago that he would never again take for granted being warm, even uncomfortably so.

"Turn around and let me check your straps for twists," said Drake as he began looking over De la Cruz' gear for any possible safety violations.

Drake checked first to see that the UDT vest was secured properly, the straps untwisted and evenly taut, tied tightly with half-hitches. He then checked the vest's manual inflation hose, signal whistle, and CO_2 actuator for any signs of corrosion or sand intrusion. It all looked spick and span. Once Drake had finished, De la Cruz proceeded to look him over quickly, with equally satisfying results.

De la Cruz gave Drake a light pat on the back and they returned to their positions in formation. Drake stood loosely at attention while he waited for some sign of instructor presence to reveal itself.

In his head he had begun, even without noticing, going through a series of mental rehearsals, as was his habit before executing any procedure.

He saw the sunlight breaking through the choppy waves and illuminating slivers of the murky Pacific water. Several varieties of seaweed were drifting in the water around him, but apart from that there was no other sign of non-human life. The Hotel Del was visible on the beach with every stroke as his head rhythmically emerged through the surface of the water to take a controlled breath.

He could feel vividly the sensation of hypothermia setting in as he approached the half-way point of the swim. His muscles were fatiguing with every pull and every kick as he hauled through the ocean the weight and drag of his equipment, but he was too cold to notice. In a few minutes, it would be almost impossible to resist the urge to tuck his arms and legs in close to his body to preserve enough warmth to stop himself from passing out, but he must keep swimming. His shivering had turned into violent, uncontrollable jack-hammering.

The taste of blood was in his mouth again. It was the surest sign that he'd contracted SIPE (swim-induced pulmonary edema, a forty-eight-hour condition believed to be caused by the combination of over-hydration, cold, and laying on one's side for too long). Once he reached the turn-around, he'd have the opportunity to roll over onto his other side for what remained of the swim, but until then, it was necessary for navigational purposes that he maintain sight of the shoreline.

He blocked the pain out of his mind, but was unsure

if he would still have the strength and coordination to combat Stokley by the time he reached him. Right now, that didn't matter. All he could do was push forward and refuse to give up. When this was all over, he'd have succeeded or he'd have failed. Either way, there was no turning back now. There never was any turning back.

Drake visualized himself reaching the green, eight-foot tall, triangular buoy that served as the marker for the half way point. Beside it sat Stokley in the small, yellow instructor kayak, directing trainees to swim down to the ocean floor forty feet below, grab a mucky, muddy soil sample, and bring it to the surface as proof. As he blew out his oxygen to make himself less buoyant, he saw De la Cruz disappear under the water and slowly begin his descent, but instead of following, he waited until he had sunk a foot under the surface and positioned himself directly under the kayak.

Drake felt himself pushing the port side upward hard with his left arm, flutter-kicking his fins powerfully to help force the kayak over. His right hand was grasping tightly the rubber grip of the dive knife.

Drake pictured the kayak rolling and Stokley's body entering the water sideways, unable to move, his legs still trapped inside the body of the kayak. He was pulling downward on Stokley's hair with his left hand to tilt the head and expose the region of the neck housing the carotid artery as he brought up the knife with his right.

"Standby!"

Drake came back to the beach and assumed a position of attention.

"Senior Chief Grand!"

"Hoo-yah, Senior Chief Grand!"

"Chief Avilez!"

"Hoo-yah, Chief Avilez!"

"Instructor Hodges!"

"Hoo-yah, Instructor Hodges!"

"Instructor Stokley!"

"Hoo-yah, Instructor Stokley!"

"Instructor Dunn!"

"Hoo-yah, Instructor Dunn!"

"269, standby for swimmer inspection!" yelled Hodges through the megaphone from atop the berm.

Drake slid the CO_2 canister out from the leg of his wetsuit and held it in his right hand while he used the left to unlatch the sheath of his dive knife and remove it. He held out both forearms in front of himself, the elbows bent at ninety degrees. In his right hand, palm open, he held the small CO_2 canister. In his left hand, palm also open, he held the dive knife, blade facing his body, tip pointed towards his bicep. He bent the tips of his fingers inward on the hilt of the knife to maintain some positive control over it for safety reasons.

Instructor Dunn, clipboard in hand, had begun walking northward from the southernmost swim-pair in the formation, checking attendance.

"Swim-pair One: Ackerman, Anderson!" Drake heard from the south end of the formation, about thirty feet from where he was standing.

"Swim-pair Two: Baker, Beck!"

"Swim-pair Three: Becton, Black!"

Hodges was following behind him, performing a quick but thorough inspection of every trainee.

"After you and your buddy have both been inspected, go get wet and sandy and then return to where you're

130

standing now!"

"After you've been inspected, get wet and sandy and come back to where you are now..."

"Swim-pair Twelve: De la Cruz, Drake!" Drake sounded off as Dunn passed him. Hodges was still a few swim-pairs down from them.

"Your knife is covered in rust. You and Clarke can drop down and push 'em out 'til I come back," Hodges said, still just out of Drake's line of sight as he threw Seaman Clinton's dive knife down into the sand, missing Clinton's foot by a fraction of an inch.

"Hoo-yah, Instructor Hodges."

When Hodges reached Swim-pair Twelve, he inspected De la Cruz first, checking to make sure all gear had been donned properly and that none of the pieces was rusted or corroded. He then turned to Drake and did the same. Hodges made no gesture or comment to indicate anything out of the ordinary.

Drake took care in resheathing his knife and inserting his CO_2 canister into the actuating device of his UDT vest. De la Cruz did the same before they each grabbed their own pairs of fins, hung them over their left wrists, and jogged down to the surf zone.

Once they were in about knee-deep, both turned to face the shore and dropped into the water backwards. Drake gasped for breath once as he popped back out of the water. The pair dumped the water out of their fins and came back into shore where they spent about twenty seconds rolling around on the beach, completely covering themselves in sand.

Drake returned to the spot where he had been standing during the inspection and grounded his fins to his left side. By now, Hodges had inspected about half the swim-pairs and Avilez, who had started inspecting trainees at the opposite end of the formation, was working his way southward.

"Raise your hand if you haven't been inspected!" yelled Dunn from the south end of the formation, where he had begun recording the pass or fail of each swim-pair.

"Raise your hand if you haven't been inspected..."

A few hands in the middle of the formation went up.

"Is there no one else?" he yelled.

The trainees glanced around at each other inquisitively for a moment, unsure whether or not Dunn was intentionally quoting Brad Pitt's line from "Troy."

"Is there no one else..." they repeated anyway, still unsure.

Drake, well insulated by the layer of mud covering him, was still relatively warm. He turned his head around and spotted Stokley in the kayak, beginning to paddle from the starting buoy to the turnaround buoy, approximately one nautical mile north. Any minute now, the class would be called into the water to form up for the start of the swim.

"School circle!" yelled Avilez from the center of the formation.

"School circle..." echoed the class as they formed a semi-circle around Avilez, facing the water behind him.

"I'd like to recap some basic points of this swim before we get started. First of all, what is the *maximum* distance you are allowed to be from your swim buddy at any time?"

"Six feet," sounded off several trainees.

"Right. Next, if you or your swim buddy hypes out or SIPEs out so badly that you can't continue and have to be removed from the evolution, what do you do?"

"Pull the actuation tab to inflate his UDT vest. Then wave a hand in the air to signal the instructor staff. If they don't spot us within five seconds, sound off using the safety whistle," said Greenwood from the back of the school circle.

"Remember also that you can bring attention to a safety hazard by signaling a training timeout. Everybody show me the signal for training timeout."

The trainees raised their right fists in the air and yelled either 'T-T-O!' or 'Training Time Out!'

"If none of the above works, just grow a pair and save yourself. Last, but not least, what do sharks like to eat?"

"Seals?"

"What do you all look like dressed up in those black wetsuits with your fins on?"

"Seals?"

"What do you do if you or your swim buddy gets attacked by a shark?"

"Stab it..." replied most of the class matter of factly.

"That sounds like a good idea to me. You've all got those well-sharpened dive knives on you, so don't be afraid to use them if necessary, but afterwards, be sure to follow standard emergency procedures."

"Hoo-yah, Chief."

"Head out past the surf zone and form up by the starting buoy. Instructor Dunn is waiting on the jet-ski. He'll tell you when to start," said Avilez as he navigated around the mass of the class and walked up the berm to join Grand, who would be observing the evolution.

"They're still organized roughly alphabetically, but we had the class O's pair up a few of the faster swimmers with some of those at the very back of the pack to pull a few more of them into the passing range," Avilez said to

Grand.

"I hope that's enough. Choppy as the water is today, they're all going to be having a rough time guiding. It'll be damn near impossible to swim in a straight line."

"Then it should be an excellent test of their skills, right Senior?"

"I suppose. If you don't mind, I think I'll stick around and watch to make sure everything runs smoothly. We're short a couple instructors today and there are no doubt going to be plenty of hype-outs on the back half of this swim."

"That's fine by me, Senior."

10

15JUN2005: One mile south of the intersection of Spruce Ave. with Hillis St., San Diego, CA.

"Sidney, you're sure you don't have a problem with my not being there for your high school graduation?"

"Don't worry about it, Dad. I'm not even planning to be there for my high school graduation. I've got better things to be doing than parading around in a used rental gown all day exchanging farewells with Malibu's teenage mediocrity, pretending I'm actually going to miss them when I leave for college in two months."

"I understand how you feel, but you'll only get to graduate from high school once."

"Thank God for that. I don't think I could handle having to go through it all over again."

"I hope that one day you'll forgive society for having forced you to suffer the indignity of public schooling."

"I'll consider it. When are you getting home?"

"I shouldn't be more than an hour or so. I've got one quick errand to run first."

"I'll probably be off to the gym by then, so I'll see you when I see you."

"I love you, son."

"I love you."

The water was soaking slowly through the legs of Drake's wetsuit. He and De la Cruz were about waist-deep in the surf zone, wading out towards the buoy.

"I'll hold you so you can put your fins on," managed De la Cruz as he took hold of Drake's UDT vest to steady him.

"Thanks," replied Drake as he removed one fin at a time from his wrist and strapped them over his feet. He then returned the favor. It would be unfortunate for one of them to lose a fin now and have to try and keep pace barefoot.

The pair began breast-stroking through the surf towards the starting line of the swim. As each wave came in, they took hold of each other and dove underwater to avoid being separated or pushed back into shore.

It had started to rain lightly since they finished their inspection. The sun was finding less and less opportunity to break through the shroud of clouds overhead. As visibility steadily worsened, the day was turning more and more into every BUD/S trainee's idea of bad swimming weather. Drake, however, interpreted the progressive loss of visibility as a progressive increase in his chances of executing Stokley's assassination unnoticed.

"Phelps, help! Get that thing off of me!" screamed Practicing Paul from about thirty yards north of Drake. Drake turned and looked in their direction without slowing his pace. He saw Phelps raise his dive knife into the air, a relatively large jellyfish hooked over the end of it.

Every trainee seemed to have his own personal fear of some aspect of the open water. Phelps' was not being able to complete his swims in passing times. Practicing Paul's was apparently jellyfish. Other trainees often said sharks or killer whales. Driscoll, however, was the only one in the class, probably in the history of BUD/S, to say the things that made him dread ocean swims most were giant squids. He complained constantly of having had dreams about such creatures emerging from 'mile-deep crevices' in the shallows bordering the Coronado beach and swallowing him whole. He swore it would happen to somebody before 269 graduated, despite Coronado's recent shortage of giant squids and mile-deep crevasses.

Phelps flung the jellyfish back towards the shore and it landed high on the beach, out of the reach of the tide. Drake had yet to see any jellyfish in this water himself, but sure enough, if there was one out here, the guy who wanted to least would be the guy to find it.

Drake turned his attention back to the green starting buoy. He and De la Cruz were only about fifteen feet from it now. There were already a few dozen swim pairs gathering about it, all making sure not to drift away as they waited for their classmates to catch up.

Drake was cooling off quickly, his wetsuit now thoroughly inundated. He led De la Cruz into the center of the pack of trainees waiting just south of the starting buoy. Once there, he took hold of De la Cruz and pulled him in close to keep warm.

They bobbed gently up and down in the water as each new swell passed under them. The rest of the class would be here in a minute and the swim would begin. It would be about forty minutes or so until Drake and De la Cruz reached the turnaround and Drake made his move.

Around them, trainees were tirelessly fidgeting and playing around with their gear, checking it over and over again to make sure everything was rigged properly. That had become habit since arriving at BUD/S. Whenever there was a spare moment, sometimes even when there wasn't, everyone would constantly be checking himself and those around him for potential rigging discrepancies or safety hazards. Not even the smallest detail went unnoticed for long.

"Okay, assholes, when I say, you and your buddy are going to swim combat sidestroke north to the green buoy, swim down to collect a soil sample, and place said sample on your head as you check in with Instructor Stokley. He'll address you by swim-pair and tell you to return, at which point you will swim counterclockwise around the green buoy and return to where you are now. You will check back in with me and I will dismiss you to return to shore after I've recorded your time," said Dunn, mounted on his jet-ski.

The pack of trainees was condensing as swim-pairs strained to get as close as possible to the starting line. Those in the rear would have to stay at the rear during the swim, circumvent the bulk of the class to get ahead, or try to force their way up through the center and risk being separated from their swim-buddies, an automatic failure.

Dunn brought the megaphone back to his mouth. "Bust 'em!"

Drake and De la Cruz, positioned at the center of the horde, would be unable to maneuver much until the clump of class 269 broke apart, but that was alright. It would be easiest for Drake to maintain his anonymity mixed in among the dozens of swim pairs compacted together around him. All of his gear was stenciled, yes, but without being within a few inches of him, it would be impossible to tell him apart from any one of the other two hundred candidates dressed in exactly the same apparel.

Drake felt the fins of the swimmers around him thud against his body hard as many of them struggled to move forward. They weren't hitting hard enough to do significant damage, just a little bruising here and there. He focused on protecting his face with one arm while he used the other to stroke through the water, doing what little evading he could.

He saw a path through the pack open up nearby, but didn't go for it. As long as there was a cushion of a few dozen trainees around him, he was right where he wanted to be. He stayed on the tail of the swim-pair directly in front of him, as close as he could get without getting kicked.

As they steadily moved forward, Drake maintained a relatively slow stroking cadence. As his head broke the surface of the water with every stroke, he could tell that De la Cruz wasn't having trouble keeping up.

They were about two hundred yards from the starting line, with about eighteen hundred to go. Drake's points of reference on the shore barely seemed to be moving and the green buoy marking the turnaround point wasn't even visible yet. Behind it would be Stokley, waiting patiently in his kayak, oblivious to what was about to happen.

'I'm coming, Stokley.'

'Where do I know that name from? Maybe it was one of my BUD/S instructors. God knows we all try to forget about them as quickly as possible. 'Instructor Drake.' No. That doesn't sound quite right.'

'Could it have been someone I served with in Iraq?

No, there were only fifteen other guys deployed there with me and they're all back here now and there's no chance we would have mingled closely enough with anyone outside our platoon for him to make that big an impression on me. The name must be from sometime before then.'

Stokley let his oar paddle softly through the water, giving it just enough push to keep himself from drifting southward beyond the buoy. The waves were just calm enough not to be flooding his boat while he waited for the faster swimmers of 269 to arrive. Most of them would no doubt be moving slower than usual today, the weather and water conditions being what they were. He hoped he wouldn't have to wait around all day before he could get out of this wetsuit and have a cold beer, but not too cold, at least not without warming himself up a little first.

Drake was still coasting along right behind whichever two or three swim-pairs happened to be immediately ahead of him at the moment. He could see the Hotel Del coming up 'in front' of him. That meant he must be within a quarter mile of the turnaround buoy. By now, he might be able to catch a glimpse of it.

He lifted his head from the water to look forward, his neck stiff from the cold. Just as he did so, a choppy wave caught him in the face. He choked for a moment, coughing up some of the water. It tasted salty, as ocean water should. He remembered the bay water as having had something of a diesely tinge to it. That is, if you were lucky enough not to catch in your mouth one of the many diapers or other assorted pieces of garbage floating adrift from the trash barges that navigated that particular route.

He regained control of his breathing and put his head back into the water, having been too distracted by the choking sensation to catch a glimpse of the buoy. The instant his face entered the water, he felt something slam into it hard. It was the extra-large size fin at the end of one of HM3 Gonzales' extra-large size legs.

Drake's eyes immediately started tearing up and he could sense his nose beginning to bleed into his mask. This was definitely not going to make things any easier.

'What was the name of that girl I was dating when I enlisted, however many years ago? Sara. Sara what? Sara Drake? No, it was Sara Drane, pronounced like Renee, but with a 'D.' She had the nerve to break up with me through a 'Dear John' while I was in boot camp, the heart-less bitch. Better boot camp, than BUD/S at least. That really would have made life suck.'

Stokley placed his oar down into the kayak at his side for the time being. The current seemed to be easing up a little. He could see the first of the swim-pairs approaching the buoy and the kayak.

"Swim-pair fifty-eight: Paul, Phelps!" they sounded off as they came to a halt six feet from the kayak.

"You guys know what to do. Go get your soil samples and put 'em on your heads."

"Hoo-yah, Instructor Stokley," the two said as they dove down.

They returned to the surface about thirty-seconds later, Phelps a little bit ahead of Paul, and placed their samples on top of their dive hoods.

"That's good enough for me. Bust 'em back to the buoy," said Stokley as he put a checkmark by each of

141

their names in his logbook.

"Hoo-yah Instructor, Stokley."

Drake's mask was now about a third of the way full of reddish fluid, but his nose seemed to have stopped bleeding for the most part.

"De la Cruz, hold up a minute. I need to clear my mask," said Drake as he slowed in the water.

De la Cruz came to a stop beside him and waited as Drake dipped his head a few inches underwater and removed his mask. He felt the salt water flow into it and sting the inside of his nostrils.

Nothing felt broken, but it would be impossible to tell for sure until they were back on dry land. Underneath the sting of the water, it was still possible for him to taste the blood at the back of his nose and throat.

The water around them was murky enough that the red tinge was hardly visible, and only for a moment until it dissipated with the flow of the surrounding waves. Drake returned to the surface to drain the water from his mask. He didn't want to blow his nose to clear it underwater and risk another nose bleed.

"Ready."

He and De la Cruz continued swimming, now less than fifty yards from the buoy. Around him, Drake could see ten to twelve other swim-pairs. They would all arrive at about the same time and clump tightly around Stokley's kayak. It was unlikely that this many trainees would all manage to maintain the requisite six foot buffer between themselves and Stokley, especially trying to maneuver around those swimmers already hovering around the buoy, waiting for Stokley to record their names, ensuring the formation of the usual ocean swim turnaround Charlie-Foxtrot.

Stokley was hurriedly recording swim-pairs as fast as he could, trying not to show that he was moving 'with a sense of urgency.' After all, he was the instructor, and they were the white-shirt trainees. Why should he have to work for them?

He found his non-writing hand massaging the scar on his left cheek. The motion had long since become habit and he often did it without even noticing whenever he was nervous. His doctor had told him the scar would fade faster if he massaged it every time he thought about it.

The mark was left by a glass shard that had gone through his cheek a couple years ago during a car crash. It was the worst of the injuries he had sustained, the rest being mostly bumps and bruises, but it had cost the passenger in the car with him the better part of his career.

That man, now Instructor Hodges of BUD/S, Coronado, had given his forgiveness as soon as he was conscious again in the hospital, but Stokley had never really forgiven himself. He just couldn't help but be a fuck-up. Getting that Trident was the only thing he had ever accomplished, and it ended up meaning the end of his best friend's career, not to mention some poor, unlucky bastard's life.

Stokley saw again the light turning red, saw again how he had tried to race across and beat the traffic headed towards the intersection from his right. He saw the flash of that beautiful, brand new Porsche nearly make it past him as the two vehicles collided.

"Swim-pair Twelve: De la Cruz, Drake!"

Drake. That had been the name of the man driving the Porsche. Drake. That was the trainee who had left in his gray Porsche 911 to get Stokley's coffee this morning.

Stokley froze for an instant, and then turned his head in the direction of the voice he had just heard, but all that was there was a mass of dozens of trainees. 'Which one was it?' They were all the same. Even behind the glass lenses of the dive masks, the only eyes he saw were Drake's. He wasn't sure if they belonged to Derek Drake or Seaman Drake.

Before Stokley knew what was happening, he was underwater. He almost managed to scream out into the ocean, but it was already too late. The last thing he saw through cloudy, ungoggled vision, was the red of his own blood beginning to tint the murky water around them.

11

"...training time out..." was audible all the way back to the beach outside the Hotel Del, where Grand and Avilez were seated in a newish, white F-250. Whistle blows from several trainees could also be heard.

"What the hell is happening out there?" Grand put on his best expression of bewilderedness. He didn't have to fake the curiosity accompanying it.

"I don't know, Senior. I think I just saw Stokley's kayak flip, but I can't tell why, not from back here. I don't see him coming to the surface."

"Sound the recall alarm and bring everyone in to shore just south of the Hotel."

The truck's siren and lights started going off simultaneously as Avilez backed the truck up a couple hundred yards. The guests at the hotel were not going to be happy, but that was the least of Avilez' worries right now.

He grabbed the walkie-talkie from the dash and began radioing his staff, first Dunn on the jet-ski, to go see what was happening, and then Peterson to bring up from the compound the emergency rescue vehicle, a lifted

Ford Excursion painted the same red as Hodges' favorite F-350.

At once, two hundred and twelve SEAL trainees changed their course and headed in towards the beach. It looked like it might be the first wave of an amphibious assault, except that nobody had any rifles, explosives, training with either, or any idea at all what was supposed to be going on.

"Here they come. Let's get out there and find out what just happened."

Grand and Avilez climbed down from the pick-up and ran towards the surf to meet the first bunch of swimmers. The lights and sirens of the truck were still operating at full-blast.

Grand spotted two trainees dragging Stokley out of the surf and onto the beach by his arms. His body hung limply in between. They let him down into the sand as soon as they were out of reach of the tide. Two more trainees not far behind them were towing in the kayak, now empty.

"Everybody, back up and give him some space!" yelled Grand as he sprinted to Stokley and knelt by him to observe the damages. It was clear that Stokley had already bled out all he was going to.

"What happened? What did this to him?" asked Avilez desperately as Grand stood up and stepped away from the body. In the distance, they could see Peterson coming in with the ERV.

"We don't know. One minute, he was sitting in the kayak recording swim-pairs, and the next, the kayak was upside down, sitting in more blood than water," replied Seaman Gilbert.

"We dragged him in as fast as we could, but it looked

like he had already stopped bleeding before we even reached the shoreline," added his swim-buddy, Ensign Greenwood.

Avilez looked down at the body. There was a long gash up the right side of his neck, extending all the way from the collarbone to the chin. It was definitely not a shark bite, or any other animal bite for that matter. By now, most of the class had come into shore and was crowded around Avilez and Grand, staring on in suspense.

"Move over, I'm going to be sick," said Seaman Branson as he vomited into the sand at his swim-buddy's feet. He covered it over with more sand before the pair moved to the back of the class, away from Stokley's body.

"OIC, LPO!" shouted Avilez.

"OIC, LPO..."

"Vickers, get into a boat-crew muster facing the water. When you have the count, come back and let me know."

"Hoo-yah, Chief.

"Boat-crew muster facing the surf!"

"Boat-crew muster facing the surf..."

Peterson pulled up in the Excursion and jumped out. He came running over to Avilez and Grand.

"What's going on?" he asked.

"We don't even know for sure ourselves."

"That looks like a knife wound going up his neck. Some of the trainees said they saw his kayak turn over during the swim."

"You think one of the trainees did this?"

"I think it may have to have been, or worse, several of the trainees. Anybody swimming around out there not

147

dressed in trainee swimwear would have stuck out like a sore thumb."

"Chief, everyone is present and/or accounted for," said Kuslidge to Avilez.

"Roger that, get back to your boat-crew and take a knee with them."

"Hoo-yah, Chief."

Peterson kept a short distance between himself and the body lying lifelessly on the beach before him. Grand was, of course, well aware of what was going on, but his task at the moment was to keep Avilez oblivious to the fact that he and Hodges had been the two who plotted Stokley's death in the first place. It shouldn't be hard. After all, who would ever suspect that any SEAL, much less a BUD/S instructor would stoop so low as to kill one of his brothers for his own benefit?

"Chief, I recommend we do something to keep the trainees warmed up while we figure out what to do next. No doubt, some of them are already starting to hype out," Peterson suggested.

"I agree with Peterson, Chief, but I think first it would be best if we confiscated all their dive knives."

"Ok, Peterson, go have everyone get sandy and then tell Petty Officer Corbin and a swim-buddy to collect their knives before you start running them through some bear-crawls and backs-bellies. I see Dunn coming into the shore now, take him with you. I don't think it would hurt for us to each be with a swim-buddy right now either."

Peterson left the chiefs and walked down to the class to start them going.

"269, Feet!"

"Feet!"

"I need MA2 Corbin and a swim-buddy!"

"Corbin and a swim-buddy..."

"Hoo-yah, Instructor Peterson," said Corbin in his usual high-pitched voice, though he sounded much more serious now. He was joined by Hernandez.

"I need you two to collect all the dive knives and line them up in boat-crews facing the surf. I want you to personally ensure that every trainee hands you his knife, stenciled with his name, and that it is grounded with his boat-crew."

"Hoo-yah, Instructor Peterson," Corbin answered as he and Hernandez ran up to the north end of the formation.

"Corbin is going to be coming around collecting everyone's dive knife. You are to remove it from your belt and give it to him, then down your UDT vests, dive masks, and fins in boat-crews where you are now."

Corbin and Hernandez began one at a time taking dive knives from the class, placing them neatly in boat-crew formation just north of the original formation.

"Once your knife has been collected, jog the formation south two hundred yards and drop down."

"Once your knife has been collected, jog the formation south two hundred yards and drop down..."

Drake was standing behind Phelps in their place in the formation, fumbling around with the straps of his UDT vest to try to get them loosened. By now, his hands were so cold he could barely move a finger without it cramping up and going completely numb. It took him until Corbin came around to collect his dive knife to undo the first strap of the vest. He left the other strap tied and managed to wriggle out of it.

"Seaman Apprentice Drake," he said as he handed off his knife to Corbin, who passed it to Hernandez to put in formation with the others. Any evidence of it having been the knife they were looking for had been washed right off by the Pacific as quickly as it appeared.

Drake wasn't thinking about Stokley now. That was in the past, and right now, Drake needed to be in the present. He locked away the image of Stokley writhing at the end of his knife for the time being. There would be a chance to bring it back out later, to savor it from the warmth and security of his rack after his last official work-day had come to an end.

Drake downed the rest of his gear and fell out to the second group of trainees forming up southward. He dropped down into the push-up position behind Phelps. He hovered there above the sand, still shivering, still too numb to feel the soreness in his pectoral muscles and deltoids. He closed his eyes and cleared his mind as he listened to the rhythm of the waves rolling into the shore.

Peterson and Dunn waited in front of the original formation until the bulk of the trainees had surrendered their knives, and then followed them south to begin what was sure to turn quickly from a warm-up into a full-intensity BUD/S beat-down.

"Senior Chief, we've got to get the police out here immediately. I'm going to—"

"Slow down a minute, Avilez. We've got to be smart about this. If word gets out to the public that there's a chink in the SEAL training chain, this place is going to go under, or at the very least be reduced to something far less than it is now, and not long thereafter, the legacy for which we and our brothers before us have sacrificed so much to develop and nurture will be destroyed. You know as well as I do that BUD/S can't afford any more bad publicity."

"Then what are we supposed to do about this?"

"We're already doing it. Call Hodges out here to help Peterson and Dunn keep the class busy while we contact the XO and the CO and figure out how they want to take care of the situation. We have to ensure that this gets handled internally."

"And what about Stokley?"

"Let's get what's left of him into the ERV before some tourist looking out the window of his suite at the Hotel Del catches drift that something's not right down here and decides to start taking pictures for the local papers."

Grand and Avilez opened the rear doors of the Excursion and heaved Stokley's corpse into it. As soon as he was in, Grand shut the doors. One of them clunked against Stokley's skull.

"Senior, don't you think we should take it a little easy on his remains?"

"Or what? We might wake him up?"

Avilez was clearly confused by Grand's uncharacteristic disrespect. "He's still a teammate, dead or alive, and I'm sure somebody's going to want that body when we're done with it."

"Avilez, by the time we're done, there won't be any body left. Get in your truck and follow me back while you call Hodges. And turn off that emergency siren."

"Aye, aye, Senior Chief," responded Avilez with the same 'aye, aye' that every Sailor uses when he obeys an order because it's an order, not because it's his first choice of action.

Avilez left Grand at the Excursion and headed back

to the F-250 they had driven in at the start of the swim.

"This is all wrong," Avilez said to himself. He understood Grand's point about handling the issue as discreetly as possible. This kind of scandal, if made public, would undoubtedly mark the end of several guys' careers in the Teams, but Avilez was beginning to worry less and less about where his career was going. He was really going to have to watch his back.

12

"Push 'em out!"

"Push-ups. Ready!" yelled Kuslidge to the class from the front of the formation where he and Vickers hovered in the leaning rest.

"Ready..." The word came out in a discouragingly dull tone. There couldn't have been any indicator more obvious to how quickly hope for a relaxing evening on liberty was fading, fading into the endless abyss of optimistic BUD/S wishes that would never see fruition.

"Down!"

"One..."

"Down!"

"Two..."

"Stop! Everybody stop!" sounded Dunn's voice from the megaphone. Drake was really getting sick of hearing that megaphone. "It looks to me like Seaman Koestler doesn't want to touch his chest to the ground on every push-up. Let's all start back over at zero for Seaman Koestler."

"Push-ups. Ready!"

"Ready..."
"Down!"
"One..."
"Down!"
"Two..."

"Sir, we tried to get a hold of the CO as well, but we didn't have any luck," said Grand to the Executive Officer.

"Don't bother trying again. He's out of town on vacation attending a change of command ceremony and won't be back until Sunday. Where is the body?"

"It's right here in the back of the truck, Sir," said Avilez as he opened the rear double doors of the Excursion for the XO to look inside. Only the odors of salt and sand emerged from within.

"Yeah, he's dead alright. Goddamn, I had hoped I wasn't ever going to have to bury another SEAL, and definitely never expected it to happen here. Senior Chief, let's go inside your office where we can talk. I don't want to risk a stray second or third phase trainee overhearing any of this."

"Down!"

"Eighteen..." Ten percent of the class was producing ninety percent of the noise. They screamed out every number as a makeshift battle cry. They counted push-up after push-up *at* Instructor Dunn. Most of those ten percent would be SEALs one day.

"Down!"

"Stop! Stop! Everybody look at HM3 Gonzales! HM3 Gonzales doesn't want to lock out his elbows at the top of every push-up! Let's all start over for HM3!"

"Push-ups. Ready!"

"Ready..."

Drake was one of the few trainees whose push-up form was still passable. His back was straight and his head was up. It was only a matter of time, though, before even he would be too fatigued to do a proper push-up.

His hands were slowly sinking deeper and deeper into the wet sand with every push-up and every arriving wave. He clenched his fists beneath the surface of the beach, feeling the mushy matter squish around in his grip. The sensation felt strangely soothing.

From behind, Drake could hear Driscoll grunting with every repetition, struggling to keep himself up. To his right was Greenwood, forcing what could have been his last ounce of strength into every push-up. There was a visibly pulsating vein running the length of his recently shaven head that looked as if it might explode out from under the skin at any moment.

"We can keep going all day long if that's what it takes for you guys to figure out how to do twenty good push-ups in a row."

"Down!"

Crowded into Grand's office was the trio of brass, trying to work out a solution based on the information on which the XO had just been briefed.

"Do we even know who did this?"

"No, not yet, Sir. Surely it must have been a trainee, or somebody mixed in with them wearing trainee swim gear, but there's no telling which one or which ones."

"Why would anybody do this to an instructor?"

"Why wouldn't anybody do this to an instructor? We spend twenty-four hours a day planning, whether it be for training's sake or not, how to make their lives miserable. Don't tell me it never crossed your mind when you passed through BUD/S all those years ago, Sir," reflected Grand from behind his own desk.

"You make a good point. You think that maybe somebody might have taken something Stokley said a little bit too personally this time."

"For all we know, the entire class is conspiring to put the instructors through their own version of Hell, but either way, I don't think that's what we need to be worrying about right now. What we need to do is figure out where to go next," said Avilez.

"Sir, I have a recommendation."

"Go ahead, Senior Chief."

"I think we should continue with the course of instruction as is. Even under the present circumstances, I don't think it would be a good idea to deviate from the original phase plan."

"Grand, we can't just move on from this. We've got to deal with it immediately and fully."

"I'm not suggesting we abandon an investigation. I'm just saying that we don't let up on the trainees. If we put the class on hold, we may very well be giving whoever is behind this exactly the break they're asking for. BUD/S must continue."

"In the meantime, while we're sorting this mess out and finding out who's done it, what's to keep them from killing their next victim tonight, or tomorrow, or whenever?"

"I don't know if there is a sure way to stop them from trying, but let's not let them forget who they're dealing with. We're the Navy SEALs. We're just going to have to step up our game a few notches," said Grand, "We'll travel armed and with swim-buddies at all times, and keep the candidates so exhausted with their training evolutions that they won't be able to fight back. I think it's important to combat the guilty parties without deviating too far from the regular course of the program and compromising all the training we've already put into the truly dedicated trainees."

"What are we supposed to do about BUD/S open DOR policy? That's a sure way out for anybody wanting to make their escape, and, come Hellweek in two weeks, it wouldn't even be at all conspicuous."

"If we absolutely have to, we can always recall anyone who leaves. They're all on record and they're all still stuck in the Navy for at until their contracts expire whether they finish SEAL training or not, which means somebody will know where they are."

"That sounds like bad reasoning and a worse plan to me. Every one of those candidates, guilty murderer or not, is being screened for his will to succeed and taught never to give up, no matter how tired or how cold he is, or how badly he hurts."

"Then I guess we had better strike now, and hard. I'll get HM1 Williams and HM1 Boyle out here right away."

13

"Hello...yes, Senior...Okay, we're on it," said Hodges into his cell phone from his post with Peterson and Dunn in front of 269's formation.

"269, feet!"

"Feet..." sounded the class unenthusiastically as they all climbed sloppily to their feet.

"Backs!"

"Backs..." They all fell lifelessly onto their backs, thudding hard into the dirt as they landed.

"Bellies!"

"Bellies..."

"This time, when I say feet, you move at BUD/S speed! You move like it is the most important thing in the world! Do you understand?"

"Hoo-yah, Instructor Hodges..."

"Feet!"

"Feet..." Every member of the class mustered up what little strength he had in reserve and popped to attention. Some prayed they were done with this session, others that they weren't. Whatever came next might be worse.

"Everybody grab your gear minus your dive knives and line up four ranks to move, facing south!"

"Grab gear minus dive knives and line up four to move south..."

Drake ran back to his boat-crew's place in the gear formation and collected what was his. He didn't bother putting any of it back on. He knew they must be getting ready to change out of their swim gear anyway.

"Hey, guys," whispered Clarke, "I think I made out the voice on the other end of the line with Hodges saying something about a level three beating."

"What's a level three beating?" asked Practicing Paul.

"It's like any other beat-down, except that they have one hundred percent of the medical staff present so that as trainees continue to collapse, they can be pulled out and treated on the spot, then sent back in to be beaten some more, without having to stop the session and give everyone else a rest break," answered Phelps.

Drake could see around him that there were still a few trainees in denial. They thought surely Clarke was wrong and they were about to jog back to the drying cages to change out, get some sort of boring proctor brief, and be secured for the day. Drake knew better. He trotted over to the easternmost rank and took his place as he waited for Hodges to start them running down to the compound. They were only about a mile away, but today that was going to be a slow, painful mile.

"Moving!" yelled Hodges from in front of the formation.

"Moving..."

14

Drake stood with the left edge of the toe of his left boot touching the last three inches of log number Two. Directly in front of Drake, stood Phelps, the rest of the boat-crew lined up in front of him. Driscoll was at the very front.

Thirty-one logs manned by thirty-one boat-crews plus one empty log encircled a portable, wooden PT platform. Each log was a chopped off segment of retired telephone pole, about a foot in diameter and ten feet long. Each weighed close to two hundred pounds dry. The platform was roughly nine feet long by nine feet wide and two feet off the deck. Nailed to the front side was a wooden cutout of the SEAL Trident logo with the words 'The Only Easy Day Was Yesterday' superimposed. Today, those immortal words would prove to be truer than ever.

At the moment, the platform was positioned at the dead center of the BUD/S obstacle course, set into the sand filling the void between the circular organization of a dozen wooden obstacles. Among them were the fifty foot cargo net climb, the slide-for-life tower, the spider wall, and others.

Present beside the PT platform were Petty Officers Williams and Boyle with the ERV. Senior Chief Grand was seated in a dusty blue F-350 outside the perimeter of the O-course. Avilez, Dunn, Peterson, and Hodges stood atop the platform itself, gathered around a makeshift wooden stand supporting 'the' bell. It would be getting plenty of use tonight. With the exception of Hodges, the entire staff looked pissed off. With the exception of Drake, so did every trainee.

"I think we all know about how this is going to go. Some bad shit happened during that swim and now all of you will pay the price. Whether it was one of you or two of you or a hundred of you, your collective fingers all pulled a collective trigger, and you will all receive collective remediation until we are confident that you are no longer capable of a repeat offense. The open DOR policy is still in effect if any of you feel like you can't handle what you've got coming to you," said Hodges through the megaphone.

One trainee from Boat-crew Eighteen stepped out from his beside his log, directly across the way from Drake and offered, "Seaman Zane, DOR." He approached the platform and stood at attention in front of Avilez.

"Well, get up here then. You know what to do."

Zane climbed up onto the platform and rang the heavy brass hammer against the cone of the bell three times.

25JAN2008: On the Grinder of the BUD/S Compound, Cornado, CA.
    "Who is the youngest member of the class?"
    "Sir, that would be Seaman Apprentice Drake. He's the only

member of the class still seventeen."

"Seaman Drake!"

"Drake..."

"Seaman Apprentice Drake, moving!"

"Drake, moving..."

"Drake, damn you're big. You're the youngest guy here?"

"Yes, Sir."

"Okay, well, anyway, as the youngest member of the class, it's tradition that I designate you the bell boy. It's nothing personal, just a seniority thing. Well, a juniority thing actually, if you want to be technical, but you get the point."

"Yes, Sir."

"The class will phase up on Monday so tonight, as soon as we break for the weekend, I need you to run into the first phase office and get the phase one bell from Senior Chief's office. Then I guess you can just polish it over the weekend with, well, bell polish, or whatever one uses for this kind of task. As long as it's hanging up on the grinder Monday looking nice and shiny, I don't care how you handle it."

"I'll take care of it, Mr. Vickers."

Drake saw several trainees urinating down their legs into the sand. It was a good idea to start off the evolution with an empty bladder, but he decided to wait until the next time they were sent into the surf zone to get wet before pissing himself.

"Before we start, let's make things just a little bit more interesting," said Hodges. Without turning his head, he fixed his eyes on Ensign Greenwood. Even though it was impossible to see them shift behind the opaque lenses of Hodges' Oakleys, the tallest member of the class knew those eyes were trained on him.

"Hey Redwood, have your shortest guy fall in with Boat-crew Two."

Greenwood directed Seaman Smith to join Two. Smith left promptly and stood in place behind Drake, just out of reach of the back of the log, which was designed to be carried by only seven men.

Hodges then hopped down from the platform and made his way out to the empty log positioned between Boat-crews One and Thirty-one before turning to face Boat-crew Two and speaking. "Seaman Drake and Seaman Driscoll."

"Drake and Driscoll..."

Drake walked up to the front of his boat-crew and joined Driscoll. The two of them ran over to Hodges and stood before him at attention. Hernandez took Driscoll's place at the front of log Two as Smith stepped forward to take the rearmost position.

"What are you two waiting for?" asked Hodges, "Get some." Hodges left them and returned to his place atop the PT platform.

Drake and Driscoll could sense the focus of the entire class on them, even though everyone was still at attention. They turned to face each other, exchanging the 'Well, this is it' look.

"Do you want front or rear?"

"I'd say we're both about to get it up the rear."

"I'll take the front. You be coxswain." Driscoll stepped up to the forward end of the log.

"Hey, Scott," said Drake from the back of the log.

"Yeah, Sid?"

"You know we're going to make this log our bitch, right?"

"Fuck yeah, we are."

The two let out a burst of boisterous laughter to fabricate a brief euphoria. A few nearby trainees shook their

163

heads in confused disapproval. 'What are those assholes so happy about?'

Hodges voice came over the megaphone once again. "Chest carry!"

"Prepare to chest carry. Chest carry," said Drake, as well as thirty-one other coxswains. He and Driscoll each wrapped one arm underneath the log and one arm over-top, then hoisted it to chest level before positioning both arms underneath the log to support it directly in front of their chests.

"Log lunges, moving clockwise around the PT platform!"

"Log lunges clockwise," said Drake, "One..." he counted as they stepped forward with their left feet and allowed their right knees to drop into the sand. "Two..." They pushed off with their right feet, returning to attention. "Three..." They stepped with the right foot this time. "Four." They came back to attention, breathing heavily, backs aching, vascularity clearly defined beneath the paper-thin skin of their biceps and forearms, exactly two yards from where they had started.

After nearly two hours of lunging circles around the PT platform, with occasional breaks to do flutter kicks, push-ups, and compound overhead movements with the logs, the class was becoming weaker by the minute. Dozens of trainees had fallen out of the evolution to receive medical treatment and emergency hydration breaks, only to be sent right back in minutes later. A few trainees had fallen out repeatedly. As far as Drake had been able to observe, nobody else had DORed since the beating started.

Boat-crew 'Thirty-two' was the only crew not to have had a member collapse from exhaustion yet.

"How are we doing down there?"

"Doing just fine. I'm so delirious it almost doesn't hurt anymore."

"I'd tell you not to let yourself die under this log but I know you wouldn't listen."

"Your wrists chafed bloody yet?"

"Yeah, they've been bleeding onto my cammies for the past twenty minutes."

Drake, lying on his back six feet from Driscoll, holding the log overhead at the end of his extended arms, looked again at the back sides of his own wrists while he continued to flutter kick. They were rubbed raw from grinding against the knees of his BDU trousers under the weight of the log during their log lunges. A single drop of blood dripped from one of his knuckles and landed just above his right eye.

"Get up and line up in ranks of four at the foot of the berm!"

"Prepare to down log. Down log," directed Drake. He and Driscoll lowered the log to their chests and rolled it down their bodies to their feet before pushing it off into the sand. They jumped to their feet and took knees to the right of the log.

"Prepare to chest carry. Chest carry to the berm," Drake called and they hoisted the log back into a chest carry yet again. They ran as fast as they could to the base of the berm, maybe ten yards from the outer perimeter of the O-course on the west side.

"Guys, I'm going to need to head out and get some sleep. I got nailed with the CDO watch tomorrow from 0400 to 1000," said Avilez as he climbed down from the

165

PT platform.

"You want one of us to walk you back into the compound?"

"No. As long as you've got everyone occupied here, I don't think it should be an issue."

"Alright. You take it easy, Chief."

Avilez surrendered his post beside the bell and bypassed the class on his way out of the O-course back to the compound.

Drake and Driscoll were the fifth boat-crew to arrive at the berm and fell into formation with the first four, beginning the second row. The other boat-crews trickled in a couple at a time over the next thirty to forty seconds. Meanwhile, all other trainees were still standing at attention with their logs in a chest carry, straining to keep them up.

When the last boat-crew, Boat-crew Nine, which currently had only three members present finally arrived, Instructor Hodges addressed the class over the megaphone again. "Down logs!"

"Prepare to down log. Down log." Drake and Driscoll set their log as gently as possible into the sand at their feet and returned to attention. The boat-crew next to them was not so considerate towards their own log. Peterson and Dunn ran down to reprimand them for not taking more care.

"Since you lazy shitbags can't even take the time to show my log a little respect, you can pick it back up and hold it at a chest carry while everyone else rests."

"Hoo-yah, Instructor Dunn," they replied wearily as they struggled to lift the log.

When Peterson and Dunn returned to the PT platform, Hodges spoke once more. "When I say 'bust 'em', the first four boat-crews are going to chest carry over the berm and down to the surf, get wet with your log, and chest carry back over the berm to the rear of the formation." Hodges looked at his watch for several seconds. The trainees in the first four boat-crews stood tensed behind their logs.

"Everyone, chest carry. First row, bust 'em!"

Boat-crews One, Two, Five, and Twenty-two exploded out of the formation and raced up the berm, pushing hard in the hope that they'd beat out the others and maybe be secured for the day.

Drake saw each pass over the top of the berm and waited as they did their business, some more literally than others, on the far side. He noticed that Grand had positioned his truck atop the berm, where he could look down on those trainees beyond it and ensure that none were cheating.

Drake heard several voices screaming in fierce, competitive agony as they reappeared over the top of the berm. It was Boat-crew One that came over first, with Two right behind.

"Boat-crew One, fall out and ground your log back where it was at the start of the evolution! Then, start a boat-crew muster in front of the PT platform!" yelled Peterson.

Greenwood gave them the command and they headed back inside the perimeter of the O-course. Boat-crew Two, as well as Five and Twenty-two behind them, returned to the rear of the formation, logs still at chest carry.

"Alright, Sid. Let's do this thing. Let's finish this right now."

"Hoo-yah," said Seaman Apprentice Sidney Drake for

the last time.

"Second row, bust 'em!"

Drake and Driscoll took off up the berm, skating their feet upward sideways to try to stop the sand from sinking out from under their heavy footsteps. In ten seconds, they were up the berm, and in another ten they were at the waterline.

"Turn us around!" The two began to walk, Drake forwards and Driscoll backwards until the log was reversed and they faced the berm.

"Prepare to lie down. Lie down." They squatted into the water and leaned back, lowering the log onto their chests as they fell into an incoming wave.

"Up!" yelled Drake as he and Driscoll heaved themselves up and out of the surf. With wet BDUs and a wet log they would have been carrying an extra twenty pounds each.

"Let's go! We're ahead!" yelled Driscoll as they headed back for the berm. They were pushing as hard as they could, but with bodies on the brink of exhaustion under the weight of their load weren't moving any faster than the average man's brisk walk as they powered across the beach.

"We're almost there! Ten more seconds!" They climbed up the berm, almost falling into it as the cumbersome log pulled their torsos forward.

The two reached the top of the berm seconds ahead of Boat-crew Three.

"Hoo-yah!" bellowed Driscoll with his last bit of wind.

Hodges and Peterson came down from the platform and approached the formation. Hodges had an IBS oar in one hand.

"Drake and Driscoll, disqualified. Line up at the

back of the formation. Boat-crew Three, down your boat and join Boat-crew One."

Hodges left Peterson's side and ran over to confront Drake and Driscoll.

"I bet you guys think you're better than everyone else now don't you?"

"Actually, Instructor Hodges, we just proved it," said Drake, still holding his end of the log at chest level.

"You want to be funny, trainee? I'll give you something to laugh about!" Hodges jabbed the handle-end of the paddle into Drake's ribcage, just below the point where the log was covering him. There was a loud cracking sound as the paddle hit.

Drake let out an audible whimper as he fell to the ground, log still in hand but unsupported. Driscoll went down with him, unable to hold the full weight of the log on his own. The two lay there as both corpsmen left whichever trainees they were treating at the moment and rushed over.

They heaved the log off the pair and HM1 Williams turned Drake over on his back. Boyle helped Driscoll get to his feet and began performing a quick examination of his vital signs.

Williams carefully unbuttoned Drake's BDU blouse so that it lay open and then cut open the front of his T-shirt to reveal several obvious breaks in the ribs. Drake lay still on the ground, groaning as he tried not to breathe any heavier than necessary.

"Boyle, this guy looks pretty beat up. I think we'd better get him to the clinic."

"Is it just the ribs?"

"I think so. I don't see any sign of internal bleeding. Let's see if we can get him up and over to the ambulance without puncturing a lung. Seaman Drake, we're going to try to help you onto your feet. See if you can stand up with us," said Williams as he and Boyle gently supported the arm on Drake's good side. He got his legs under himself and stood up the rest of the way.

Williams instructed Driscoll to take a knee by Boatcrews One and Three and then led Drake over to the red Excursion to drive him the remaining two hundred yards to the BUD/S medical clinic. Their log lay where they had left it. It would be somebody else's problem.

15

Drake sat silently in the waiting room of the medical clinic. He was alone except for the Seaman working the reception desk. Drake recognized him as being a member of the class ahead of his, 268. 'He must be a dropout fishing for a recommendation to get put into the corpsman training pipeline.'

Drake had already been examined and was waiting for an official decision from the doctor on which path his training would take, though it was obvious the damage was more than enough to warrant a medical separation.

After a time, a tiny oriental man with very little hair, all of it gray, emerged from the depths of the clinic wearing a white coat. He looked ancient and frail, like maybe he had been the doctor who did the physicals for the candidates of BUD/S class One over four decades ago. If so, he would have looked old then too, Drake suspected.

"Seaman Apprentice Drake," he said in surprisingly mediocre English.

"Seaman Apprentice Drake," responded Drake, coming to attention as gently as was manageable.

"Seaman Drake, as you can see from this x-ray of the right side of your ribcage," said the man whose upside-down nametag read 'Dr. Phay' as he pointed to an x-ray of Drake's teeth, "the damage is rather extensive. It will take at least eight weeks to heal if I put you on complete bed-rest. I have no choice but to recommend your immediate medical removal from training." Dr. Phay spoke without emotion, as he undoubtedly had to hundreds of trainees before Drake in decades past. He closed the dental record folder and handed it, along with Drake's medical record (which Drake assumed would contain an x-ray of his battered ribcage), to Drake before returning to whatever task had him occupied before Drake's arrival.

"I understand, Sir," answered Drake solemnly as he turned and walked slowly, reluctantly, pitifully out of the clinic. He almost managed to squeeze a tear out of one eye. It was a performance that would have inspired stray puppies the world over.

He put on his soft cover as he stepped outside, tucking the '269' hard cover under his left arm. To the west, he could see the sun beginning to set. He imagined that about this time, the class would be finishing up another beat-down session and getting sent off to chow to refuel before the next one. There would be no shortage of pain or suffering for class 269 tonight. He took a painfully deep breath of clear Coronado air and started walking across the parking lot to the CBH. He really wasn't looking forward to climbing either flight of stairs.

Senior Chief Grand finished counting, bill by bill, the money that was to be the payment for Stokley's execution. He rubber-banded each of ten stacks of five hundred, one-hundred dollar bills before tossing them into the standard-issue seabag he had purchased from the NEX across the highway earlier that day. He had been tempted to take a little extra for his own efforts, but decided against it. "This money, stolen or not, is payment for the death of a man who is a threat to everything the Teams stand for," he had said to reassure himself. 'Well, almost everything, anyway.' Even if he had helped plan Stokley's demise partly for his own gain, Grand wouldn't have felt right deceiving his brothers any more if it wasn't going to benefit them in some way. It would be payment enough for him just to move on with the rest of his life without having to be in a constant state of worry over the mistakes he'd made in the past.

Grand dropped the bag to the floor in the corner of his office and slid open the top drawer of his desk. He eyed the contents: one can of black shoe polish, one white T-shirt, partially stained with polish, one loaded, nine millimeter Sig Sauer P226, safety engaged. He left the pistol alone for the moment and removed the polish and T-shirt.

He sat down and propped his feet up on the edge of the desk so that he could reach them comfortably. He opened the can of polish and pressed the tips of his right index and middle fingers, wrapped with a segment of the T-shirt, into it. He rubbed them around in the can for a few seconds to draw out an amount of polish and then began smearing it over all the leather surfaces of each boot.

He covered up the previous coat with a fresh layer of polish, replacing the shine with a hazy dark gray, as was his practice before beginning any event that would require practical usage of the boots, not just a pretty appearance. The hard, buffed undercoat would still protect the leather from corrosion of salt and other such substances, but wouldn't reflect through the unfinished outer coat. Today he hoped this was more out of habit than necessity.

He opened the desk drawer once more and put back the polish and T-shirt. He looked down at the pistol. There wasn't really any need for it. He knew there was no unpredictable trainee threat even if nobody else did. He hesitated for a moment, then removed the gun from the drawer anyway and checked to verify that it was loaded and a round was chambered before slipping it into the leg pocket of his BDU trousers. 'Better safe than sorry,' he decided, also out of habit.

Drake stopped outside his room to remove his boots and all his clothing but the wet, black briefs he had been wearing since before the swim. He took as much care as possible working around not only his battered ribcage, but also the countless bumps, bruises, scrapes and chafes he had collected throughout the day.

He was missing big chunks of hair from regions of his legs, and the skin of parts of his groin and underarms was rubbed raw. Some of the calluses from his palms had torn off during the IBS surf passage, and some more during the log PT. The toe of one of his socks had been stained with blood, but Drake couldn't tell which toe it had come from because they all looked bloody now. Maybe all of them were bleeding.

He tiptoed as nimbly as a man in his condition could into his room to get a trash bag for his clothing and boots. After placing them inside, he tied the bag off and threw it into the bottom of his locker. He took out his shampoo and towel, and slipped on his shower shoes. He walked painfully, but dutifully, all the way back down to the head and into the shower before he collapsed onto the tile floor. It was already warm with shower water. Drake looked up to see Seaman Zane.

"Hey, Drake."

"Hey, Zane." Drake pulled himself into a seated position and leaned back against the wall of the small shower room.

"What are you doing in here?"

"Just taking a shower, you?"

"I mean, why aren't you with the class? Did you get med-rolled?" asked Zane as he looked down at the wrapping about Drake's midsection.

Drake pointed to the wrap. "Med-dropped."

"I'm sorry to hear it," said Zane. He really did look sorry, even ashamed, ashamed that he had given up voluntarily what he supposed Drake wanted badly enough to go through so much pain for.

"Don't be. I'm not. This was one of the risks and we all knew it when we signed up."

"I wouldn't say 'all' of us."

"Oh?"

"I told my recruiter I wanted to be a scuba diver and he told me this was the place to learn. How was I supposed to know I'd have to go through Hell first?"

The two chuckled for a minute. That sounded about like the typical recruiter story. Drake looked up at Zane again. "What made you stick around so long when you found out the truth?"

"I guess at first I just didn't want to quit, having to go home a failure in the minds of all my friends and family. I didn't want people to think I'd failed. Before long, though, it got to the point where I *almost* started to enjoy the stuff we were doing: lots of PT and a chance to prove ourselves every day. Right now I'm in the best shape of my life, sort of." Zane couldn't help but notice the ring of skin chafed away from his waistline as he eyed his flexing abdominal wall. The muscles would last longer than the injuries accompanying them, for the most part.

"You're not exactly quitting, you know. You're still legally attached to the Navy. You'll probably be given the opportunity to reclassify into the Navy Diver rate if you want, and that'll get you straight to dive training."

"Not a chance. I'm going to do whatever it takes to get back to BUD/S the fastest, and that usually means going to 'the fleet' undesignated and unrated. I've already decided to resubmit my BUD/S package the day I become eligible."

"Good for you. You're a better man than I am." Drake stood up slowly and removed his trunks to rinse the salt and sand out of them.

"You're not coming back?"

"No. I think I had enough fun this time around to last me for a while."

"What are you going to do then?"

"Since my separation was for medical reasons, I've got the option of being medically discharged from the Navy. It's a tempting enough offer that I may just take it." Drake was starting to lather up. For a few seconds, the shampoo stung every one of the nicks and chafes covering his body. It was his turn to show the bitch face, just a little.

"And then you'll go back to college?"

"I suppose so. I don't especially have anything better

to do. There'll be time to think it over while I'm waiting for my out-processing paperwork to go through."

Drake finished rinsing off and turned off his shower head. He stepped out of the shower and began to dry himself carefully. He paid special attention to any open cuts or chafes. "Pat your wounds dry," his father had told him. There was no point in rubbing them right back open just as they were starting to heal.

"If you need any help taking your gear over to the depot to return it, I'm in room 210."

"Thanks for the offer, but I'll probably just drive it over in the morning."

"Alright, have a good night, Drake. I'll see you across the street at X-Div."

"See you." Drake didn't mention that he had no intention of living in the X-division barracks. By now it would be full of former BUD/S and SWCC trainees who were in the midst of celebrating the relaxed grooming and cleanliness standards, or who were just too depressed to care about uprooting the roach infestation. He'd make sure to stop in before he left town to see who was still hanging around, but not until after he got settled into his usual villa at El Cordova Hotel, a mile or so north in the heart of Coronado.

Drake wrapped the towel around his waist and headed back up to his room. He felt somewhat restored by the shower. He usually felt somewhat restored after getting himself cleaned and warmed and dried at the end of a long day. He bet that by the time he removed the wrap around his still unwashed torso, it was going to smell worse than the fly-swarmed kelp clusters lingering out in the surf zone on the other side of the berm.

§

When he made it back to his room, Drake carefully slipped out of his towel and into his polypros. It hit him all of a sudden how hungry he was. He hadn't eaten since lunch. He went over to the mini fridge across the room from his bed and opened it to reveal a fresh gallon of reduced-fat milk and an unopened box of double-stuffed Oreo cookies. He and Jones usually went through one of each every weeknight. It looked like Drake was going to be getting a head-start tonight.

As he snacked, he thought about Stokley, and about his father. Drake wondered what his father would have thought about his vengeance. Would he have been proud? 'No.' Derek Drake never would have wanted his son to be put in harm's way on his behalf. Seaman Drake's father would have wanted him to let it go and move on and live his own life. There was nothing worth having to be gained by killing Stokley.

But Sidney Drake hadn't done this for his father. He hadn't done it for anyone other than Sidney Drake.

'I do this for myself.' He mouthed the words. That would be acceptable for his father, he tried to convince himself.

The man who had killed his father was dead now, but work wasn't over yet. Tomorrow would be a new day with a new task, a new challenge, and Drake would have to be ready to meet it with the same crippling success as he had today's.

He put the milk, knowing Jones wouldn't mind that it had been drunk straight from the carton, and the Oreos back where he had found them and made his way over to his rack. Thank God it was the bottom rack.

Tonight he climbed under the covers, leaving the sleeping bag folded and stowed away in his locker. He lay on his back trying not to move, but his entire torso still ached and throbbed. In spite of it all, he shut his eyes and drifted off before he had time to realize he was trying.

"Up."

"Eight..."

"Up."

"Nine..."

"Up."

Drake woke up in his rack. Was he dreaming again? 'Not this time.' He was consciously aware of the aching in his ribs. 'They couldn't still be going out there, could they? Who cares?' Drake shut his eyes again.

"Hey, Drake, open up!" came Jones' voice from outside their room. It was accompanied by the sound of his boot banging into the base of the door. "Open up. My key's broken again!"

Drake put his left hand on the metal frame of the rack overhead and lifted himself up. The frame dug into the tender skin of his palm as he pulled downward. "I'm coming." It hurt to say the words, it hurt to breathe, but mostly it just hurt.

After what seemed like miles, Drake reached the door and pulled it open. He heard the deadbolt slide open as he turned the handle. 'Oops. I guess that's why his key wasn't working,' Drake thought. He must have thrown it last night when he went to bed. He always slept sounder when the door was bolted.

Jones fell into his arms as the door opened. Drake grunted in pain as he caught him, mostly with his good side, and lowered him gently to the floor of the hallway, still trying for Jones' sake not to get the precious floor of their dorm room dirty. "Easy on the ribs, Jones."

"Did Seaman Drake just address me without sayin' 'Sir?'"

"Don't get too used to it. I'm out of here tomorrow."

"No way. They drop you?"

"Yeah they did. What's wrong with you?"

"Look aroun', Drake. 'Bout half the class just got secured. The rest will be comin' in over the next few minutes I guess. It's almost two o'clock in the mornin'."

Drake peered down the hallway in both directions. He saw some downed gear lying here and there, and some downed trainees lying here and there. One trainee was trying to open the door to his room with a credit card.

"Take a minute to catch your breath and I'll help you get down to the head."

"No, you're not in any better shape than I am. I'll work my way down there eventually. Just leave the door open."

"Will do," said Drake as he propped the deadbolt open to keep the door from closing.

"Drake, I picked up your dive knife and your swim gear for you on the way back in. If you're getting dropped you should probably take it over to Supply first thing."

Drake accepted the clear plastic bag containing his gear from Jones and took it back to his locker. He opened it and reached inside to make sure nothing was missing before placing it on the floor of his locker, next to, but not touching, his inspection boots. The locker had no personal belongings in it. All those he had kept stowed in the trunk of his car.

He made sure to close and lock his locker, having

left the room door propped open, and then slid back into bed, back under the covers, and slept.

In room 217, located directly underneath Drake and Jones', there was the sound of a tarp ruffling as Greenwood shook it open onto the floor, creating a palate for his and his lagging bunkmate's muddy boots. He hadn't turned the lights on yet, but he hadn't needed to. His room was exactly as Spartan as every other in the CBH, and laid out exactly the same that it had been since the building's erection.

He stepped onto the tarp, uneasily but carefully, worried that the fatigue might cause him to lose his balance and fall. He just hoped he would land on the tarp if it came to that. With one more step he reached the center of the tarp, and lowered down slowly, dropping to his knees before easing his hands down in front and then rolling over into a semi-seated position.

He tilted his head forward to let his hard cover fall forward off his head and then lifted a single arm up to unclip his web belt and let it too fall onto the tarp beneath. He doubted he'd be able to remove his blouse, stiff still from being coated in sand even after just having run through the de-con showers outside, without help so he started elsewhere.

"Boots, socks, pants," he whispered to himself, reflexively reversing the order in which he always put them on. For cold, blistered fingers, undoing the laces was the hardest part, until it came time to undo the buttons on the fly of his trousers. The thought of quitting still hadn't crossed his mind, but it would before he became a SEAL.

§

In room 101, LTJG Vickers collapsed in one great sandy, salty, soaking heap onto the floor of his room, boots still hanging out into the hallway. He ignored the protests of the Neanderthal who had entered the room just before, making an immense effort to tip-toe across the already grimy floor to keep from placing even more muddy boot prints on it than there already were.

'What's the point anyway?' Nathan Vickers asked himself as he felt the muck on the front of his utility blouse grinding on the floor beneath. 'They can't expect us to run this whole class day and night and still have time to keep the room looking perfect. It's not possible.' He raised his head to look at Kuslidge, no longer talking, just staring back and shaking his head to express something between disappointment and absolute disgust.

At that moment Vickers remembered his last day of leave before indoctrination had started, shaking his father's hand in the airport terminal while the final boarding call was sounded for his flight.

05JAN2008: Baltimore Washington International Airport, Maryland.
"The seven years I spent in the Teams were the best of my life, and I'd still be in if I could be. So would your grandfather. There's nothing I want more than to see you carry on that legacy. Watching you become a SEAL is going to be the proudest day of my life."

"I know it will, and I can't wait for the day that I too will get to lead Navy SEALs into battle."

"Soon enough, Nathan, you're going to have your chance, but first you have to prove yourself, and that starts right now, at BUD/S."

"You don't have to worry. They can freeze me, they can deprive me of sleep, they can run me all day long, but they can't make me quit. I'm going to make the best damned OIC they've ever seen."

Vickers couldn't help but think about what it would be like seeing his father again after he'd washed out, doubted and given up on by his own LPO. He could almost hear the tone of humiliation in his father's voice as he tried explaining to a menagerie of relatives and family friends that his only son had failed his country during a time of war. He imagined seeing his father truly ashamed of him for the first time in his life, and started to cry. Kuslidge ignored him and began undressing.

Next door in room 102, LTJG Call, already clean and dry, was seated on his rack in a pair of sweatpants, reading over the schedule of instruction for the approaching training day as he massaged his left calf with one hand. AO2 Dwayne entered the room wearing a towel around his waist and a pale-gray U.S. Navy hoodie-sweater.

"What'cha readin', LT?" asked Dwayne in a tired, but optimistic tone.

"Tomorrow's schedule. It looks easy enough, but then again, so did today's until the ocean swim incident." Call held out the paper, offering it to his ALPO.

"Thanks, but I'm alright − breakfast, probably with a beating afterwards, conditioning run, intro to rock portage. We can worry about the specifics when−" Dwayne's words were cut off by Chief Avilez, standing in the doorway in the khaki service uniform he'd be wearing on watch. He didn't wear it as well as he did the BDUs, but even if he had it would have been strange to see him out of his usual working uniform. His presence felt somewhat more human without the Oakleys and the blue-and-gold T-shirt.

"You can worry about the specifics right now because starting tomorrow the two of you are going to be the OIC and LPO of this class." The pair started to stand up, embarrassed that they hadn't already been at attention when the SEAL Chief entered the room.

"Relax, don't get up. And don't worry about calling a formation to spread the word tonight. You'd just be getting everyone all riled up for no reason. I'll notify the rest of the class, including Vickers and his boyfriend, tomorrow during breakfast.

"By the way, Seaman Drake is getting med-dropped for broken ribs so make sure to take him off the roster." Avilez turned and left as suddenly as he'd come.

"Congratulations, Sir," declared Dwayne, as much to himself as to Call. There was still a trace of optimism in his voice, but it was forced optimism. Both men sighed heavily.

Hodges slipped into the first phase office unnoticed. With the exception of Grand who was waiting for him inside his office, the rest of the staff, including medical personnel, was still busy sending off the remaining trainees in the last few minutes of their final evolution. Hodges opened the door to Grand's office and entered.

"Hey, Hodges, come in. That's a long day, huh?"

"Stokley probably thinks so."

"He's out of the picture now, for good. His incompetence has already killed one innocent man, and effectively ruined your career as a SEAL in the process. He was a waste of life and now we've dealt with him. I'm about ready to move on and leave all this behind us."

"It's not quite over, Senior. There's still the issue of tomorrow morning. I guess it's this morning now, isn't it?"

"Don't worry about that. I'll handle the money and make sure it ends up where it needs to be. Why don't you go get yourself some sleep, Hodges?"

"Aye, aye, Senior Chief."

Hodges promptly left the office, but not to head off to bed. He wouldn't sleep tonight. He couldn't have if he'd tried. That had always been one of his shortcomings. Tonight was just as big a night for him as it was for Drake and Grand. It was the start of his next life, a life of his own. He would spend tonight looking forward to tomorrow.

16

Drake could hear the waves rolling in outside, no more than seventy yards from where he slept. The sun was beginning to peer into the room through a partially opened curtain. His window was latched shut and refused admittance to the fresh aroma to which he usually awoke. The room smelled the smell of wet, sweaty sand, and stale piss.

Drake carefully pulled himself out of bed and walked over to his alarm, worried at first why it hadn't gone off. He looked down at it.

The display read 0547. He had woken up before his alarm for the first time in weeks, and today he was still the last to wake, with the possible exception of Zane and whoever else might not have made it through the previous night with the rest of the class.

Drake checked his various wounds, making sure nothing had healed on him overnight. Nothing had. He'd worry about them later. Right now, it was time to work.

Ideally, Supply would open at 0715 and it had to be the last stop he made in his checkout because they would confiscate his room key and legitimate credentials of residency at the compound. He had until 0800 to get his things packed, delivered to Supply, get dressed up and make his way back down to the drying cages to deal with Grand. He hoped Supply would be open on time.

Drake ignored the filthy, stinking bag he'd left sitting in the corner of the room last night. He went instead to his wall locker and put on his inspection uniform, with inspection cover, all starched perfectly stiff, and his inspection boots, all leather surfaces shined to mirrors. It had passed every inspection through which he'd worn it.

It was 0615 now. Senior Chief Grand would surely be back in the office, ready to start the day all over again. Drake left his room with nothing but his uniform, ID card, and room key, and walked down to the grinder.

He passed the bell, now returned to its original post on the grinder, right outside the first phase office. It still looked just as shiny as it had four days ago when he hung it up, in spite of having had some use. Lined up on the pavement to the right of it, he saw about a dozen more green 269 hard covers than had been there before. Zane hadn't been the only one to have a moment of weakness last night.

Drake came to attention at the door to the office and clanked the bell one time before speaking. "Seaman Apprentice Drake to check out."

"Get in here, Drake," said Grand from his desk indifferently. Drake entered and walked back to Grand's office. The Senior Chief looked tired.

"Good morning, Senior Chief."

"Drake, why don't you sit down? This will only take a minute."

Drake took the seat across from Grand and accepted

a pen and brief checkout sheet.

"Go ahead and fill that out. It should be pretty self-explanatory. Remind me again why you're being med-dropped."

"I fell and broke three ribs during log PT."

"That's what I thought. It's a shame accidents like that happen. As your contract guarantees, you'll be offered the chance to discharge medically with no penalty if I'm not mistaken."

"You're not mistaken, Senior Chief," said Drake as he passed the form back to Grand. Grand turned around in his chair to place it in the filing cabinet where it would likely be left to rot for eternity without ever being looked at again, just like the thousands of BUD/S separation forms already contained within. Grand didn't notice Drake remove from under the desk the palm-sized audio recorder he'd left there last Friday night while he was retrieving the bell.

"Supply will collect your room key and remove the Special Warfare identification sticker from your ID when you turn in your gear."

Grand gave his farewell to Drake with the same semi-sincere good wishes he planned on giving the next hundred guys who would leave the class before the end of Hellweek. Drake caught a glimpse of the brand-new seabag sitting in the corner of the office, but seemed to pay it no more mind than any other trainee would any other seabag.

Drake walked back to his room and folded up everything (minus what soiled pieces still rested in the bag of gear he'd worn the previous day) for which he was accountable: four sets of BDUs with one belt, two soft covers, one hard cover, one pair of boots, one set of swim apparel, and one dive knife. He would be allowed to keep the T-shirts, undershorts, socks, and one pair of boots. He would make sure to keep the pristine inspection boots and hand in the ratty, salty, sandy, torn up pair he'd been mistreating for the past month. The sleeping bag and first-aid supplies he left in the locker for the next candidate. He'd have an opportunity to use it before he graduated, or DORed.

Drake managed to fit everything into one more jumbo-sized garbage bag and grimaced from the pain in his torso as he swung it, along with the bag of dirty gear from the day before, over his left shoulder. He turned out the lights and closed the door as he left the room. The microwave clock read 0705.

The walk to the supply depot was about a quarter-mile. Drake saw one more trainee up ahead of him, but didn't try to catch up. There was still time to spare and the company just wasn't worth the effort today.

He reached the depot a few minutes later and saw that it was HM3 Sanders who was also there returning his gear. Drake didn't have a chance to speak to him before a supply clerk approached.

"You turnin' in your stuff, too?"

"Yes. Except what I'm wearing, it's all in these bags."

The clerk looked inside the larger of the two bags first, without taking an exact inventory except to make sure it had the dive knife and the hard cover. He opened the bag with Drake's unwashed BDU's next.

"What's all this shit?"

"One set of cammies, canteen and web belt, and one pair of boots."

"Whatever, smartass. I'll sort it out later."

Drake removed the BDU he was wearing and, dressed in his T-shirt and black tri-shorts, began to put his shiny inspection boots back on. He saw Sanders do the same as he finished handing in his gear. The clerk called Sanders over to where he and Drake were standing.

"You two look like a couple of clowns. You're gonna have to put on some regular uniforms before you check in at X-Division. I'll walk you out to the gate."

He collected room keys from Drake and Sanders, and then peeled the round, yellow Special Warfare compound stickers from their ID cards. He locked the gate behind them as they stepped out and returned to the supply warehouse.

"Do you need a ride across the street?" Drake offered. He didn't especially want to take Sanders anywhere at the moment, but he didn't want to be stuck here with him either.

"No thanks. One of my SWCC buddies said he'd drive me over. They've got the day off of training today."

"Alright. I guess I'll see you over there." Drake was grateful for the convenience.

"Later," replied Sanders as he turned and headed north up to the SWCC compound.

Drake walked straight to his car, parked about half-way between the gate from which he'd just come and the main entrance to the compound, out of the line of sight of any of the compound video surveillance. He opened the trunk and took out the spare set of BDUs he'd procured from supply during gear issue, as well as the extra cover, canteen belt set, and dive knife. He took them into his car and began putting them on quickly. All the outer layers he was wearing were stenciled with the name 'REED,' a convenient anagram of 'DRAKE' for which he could use his own stencil.

Once he was dressed, he reached into the glove box and pulled out a pad of round, yellow smiley-face stickers. He stuck one to his ID and examined it. It definitely didn't look like a Special Warfare sticker, but at a glance, an uninterested watch-stander might not notice.

When he was satisfied with his appearance, Drake dropped the sheathed dive knife into the right leg pocket of his trousers. He climbed back out of the car and began walking toward the main quarterdeck entrance. He dragged his feet as he walked to scuff the shine off his boots so they wouldn't stand out. He looked down at the time on his watch: 0748. He'd be coming in right behind the rest of the class as they were leaving, assuming they were relatively close to being on time.

That reminded him. Except for the OIC and LPO, BUD/S trainees weren't permitted to wear watches during the workday. He took his off and dropped it into the other leg pocket of his trousers.

He opened the glass quarterdeck door and stepped inside onto the smooth marble floor. Behind the reception desk sat two mid-twenties trainees (probably from BUD/S class 267 or 268, Drake guessed) in exceptionally well-maintained dress blue uniforms. One of them was holding the desk phone to his ear while the other leaned in close to try to hear what the semi-feminine voice on the other end of the line was saying. Both were grinning.

Drake pulled his ID out and held it so that his hand covered the better part of the smiley-face sticker as he briskly walked by, giving the trainees seated behind the desk his best attempt at a combination of the usual bewildered, first phase trainee look and the look of somebody who thought he was supposed to be here.

The trainee not on the phone waved him through without even looking at the ID, straining to make out what was being said through the telephone.

'Fine Navy watch-standing at its best,' acknowledged Drake. It would mean both their asses if it was ever discovered that they'd let a vengeful serial killer cross over into their sphere of responsibility, but Drake doubted and hoped, for his sake more than theirs, that it wouldn't be an issue.

He pushed open the door on the other side of the quarterdeck and stepped out onto the east side of the grinder. No staff members or trainees were visible, but he decided to move at a shuffle anyway, as was required of any trainee wearing the BDUs, during or after the work-day. The bouncing motion on his ribcage had him in agony, but he sought consolation from one of Instructor Peterson's favorite insights: "You can make it through anything we throw at you throughout BUD/S if you just follow one rule: Don't be a pussy." That sure had proved helpful during his first day of underwater knot-tying...

Drake saw the class' gear downed in boat-crews outside the drying cages. The trainees were nowhere to be seen. 'Maybe they're going to make it to their run on time after all.'

Drake didn't waste any time as he made his way around the downed gear to the drying cage door. He punched the combination he'd gotten from Hodges, 2-2-6-9, into the keypad and the door unlatched. As he entered, he shut the door behind him.

The sunlight was peeping in and out of the clouds

and peering through the chain link walls of the cages. There was enough gear lining the cubbies of the outer walls to keep the natural light level relatively low, but not enough to block it out entirely. There was an overhead fluorescent light, but Drake had left it off.

Every compartment but his, which contained only a life-vest and an empty seabag, still had a seabag full of swimwear. The other trainees checking out today would have to wait until later to collect their things when the class leadership unlocked the cages for them.

Drake's locker was located on the north wall, at the north end of the room. He took the seabag from inside and balled it up so it could be stuffed, just barely, into the trouser leg pocket with his watch. He turned around to examine the room from this position. It wouldn't be hard to find cover amongst all the storage compartments, but he needed a spot close enough to his locker that he'd be able to subdue Grand without having to sprint halfway across the room to reach him.

Drake stepped around several shallow puddles of water forming underneath dripping seabags as he made his way to the far side of the waist-high cubby array dividing the room in half lengthwise. He walked around the northeast corner of the array and looked towards his locker. It was a distance of about three yards. He ducked partially into the cubby at his side. It faced east, so he wouldn't be visible from the west and only entrance of the cages.

He could smell a moldy stench rising out of the seabag sharing his hiding place. Out of curiosity, he checked the stencil on it: 'GONZALES.' 'Gonzales, you relentless pig, even now, from miles away on your conditioning run, you've still managed to find a way to make yourself a nuisance.' Drake told himself he'd let it slide this time.

Then, coming from outside the drying cage, Drake first heard footsteps, and as the footsteps stopped, the electronic bleeping of the keypad. He counted silently to himself the keystrokes, 'two-two-six-nine.'

The door whined that rusty, high-pitched whine that old metal gates do and then the footsteps were inside the cages. Drake could feel his heart rate rising as they came closer and closer and closer. They stopped, not more than three yards from him.

Drake, dive knife in hand, swung around the corner and thrust into the neck of the giant, BDU-clad man standing at his locker. Well, not his locker, but the locker adjacent to it, he noticed as he withdrew the knife.

Drake recoiled back from the figure as explosively as he'd lunged at him a moment ago. It fell to the floor with one hand clutching at the back of the neck where the knife had entered, and with the other at the front of the neck where the tip of the blade had pierced all the way through. After a moment it was still.

Drake didn't have to look at the nametag on the BDU top to identify the man as Dwayne, one of four trainees other than Drake to have the combination to this room. Drake hadn't seen his helmet among those lying on the grinder.

'He must have been medically rolled or dropped this morning and come right in from medical to collect his things,' Drake saw as the only possibility.

Maybe for the first time in his life, he felt completely without direction. His mind instantly began working a hundred different angles at once, trying to figure out what to do next. Before Drake had time to make a choice, Grand appeared in front of the entrance, seabag in hand. He looked first at Dwayne's body on the floor, and then

194

up at Drake, still grasping the bloodied dive knife.

They made eye contact for a fraction of a second, and then both flew into action. Grand was turning the corner of the drying cage as Drake reached the doorway. He was moving as fast as he could manage back past the north wall of the CBH and over the grinder to the quarter-deck. Drake was right behind him and gaining fast.

Grand was reaching for his right leg pocket, fumbling frantically to undo the buttons and free the pistol still waiting inside.

"Trainee, help! I'm being attacked!" he yelled at the same time in the direction of the quarterdeck entrance.

Drake caught him and jumped on his back, not even waiting until they hit the ground to start working the dive knife in and out of his torso. He thrust repeatedly and then targeted Grand's neck. Grand struck back several times with his fists and elbows, not having had time enough to draw his sidearm, catching Drake in the face and sore side of his chest. The two rolled around in entanglement for a few seconds, stuck in each other's holds until Grand had bled out too much to function and Drake broke free. He scrambled to his feet and grabbed the seabag from what was left of the figure lying on the pavement.

Fifteen yards ahead, he could see into the quarter-deck, one trainee looking out the window at him and yelling while the other hurried to pick up the phone and dial. Drake ran straight towards the glass door facing from the quarterdeck into the grinder and smashed through it, not even breaking stride as he bolted by the watch-standers and did the same through the next door. He ignored the throbbing pain coming from his torso.

He was moving towards his car and reaching for his

keys with his spare hand, not paying any mind to the glass shards covering his BDU and scalp.

Behind him, he could still hear the one trainee screaming, "He's getting away, call the CDO! I'll get in the duty van and run him down!"

Drake reached the Porsche and unlocked the driver side door with a click of his electronic key. 'The Hell you will, shipmate.' There may come a day when, under just the wrong pair of drivers, a four-cylinder minivan can keep pace with a top of the line Porsche, but this wouldn't be it.

He hopped inside and tossed the seabag with the money onto the passenger seat. He seemed to have lost the dive knife somewhere along the way, so he dropped the sheath out the door before closing it. He turned the key in the ignition and the engine rumbled promisingly, as it always had.

The squeal of the tires on the pavement was clearly audible as Drake floored the pedal out of the parking space. He had made sure to 'combat park' so he wouldn't need to back out if he had to leave in a hurry, but this wasn't quite what he'd had in mind.

Drake was speeding down the lot towards the gate. There would be an armed rent-a-cop manning it, but there was no roadblock and wouldn't be any time for him to react before Drake was long past. In his rearview mirror, he could see the white duty van creeping up to the twenty mile-per-hour mark.

The Porsche made a hard right, nearly coming off the right side wheels as it positioned to run for the final twenty yards before the highway. Drake floored the pedal again and sent the car shooting forward past the guard shack. He hit the only speed bump in his path and was airborne for a moment.

At the intersection marking the entrance to the compound, he made another hard right, just missing a pack
of oncoming cars. He was racing southbound on Silver
Strand Boulevard, Highway 75, towards what was in his
panicked mind, the nearest out from a rapidly worsening
situation: the Mexican Border. From Mexico, there would
be a constant stream of flights able to take him into
Panama to redeem the bearer share certificate resting two
feet away in the glove box.

Panama would have to be a sufficiently secure hide-
out while he tried to figure out his next move, though at
this point it was impossible for Drake to know whether
or not there would be a next move, now that he would be
unable to return to the United States, and risked Britain
extraditing him if he chose to take advantage of the citizenship he still held there.

It would be no more than ten minutes from the
compound to the border at the speed Drake intended on
driving, and mostly over straight, flat highway. That didn't
make the circumstances any more comfortable for Drake.
He had fouled up the final play of an otherwise flawlessly
executed scheme, not to mention battered his body so
badly over the last few months that it would take the next
year to fully recover.

Drake's head was clear of any thought. Instinct
had taken over and he was fleeing as fast as he could.
Nobody was chasing him yet as far as he could tell, at
least nobody apart from the Sailor in the duty van, but it
wouldn't have made any difference to him if they were.
He felt as if the whole world were suddenly onto him,
and, as far as he was concerned, they would be soon
enough. The Porsche was known to everyone on base,

and wouldn't have been missed by anyone who saw it speed out from the compound.

The speedometer read a hundred and twenty-five miles per hour and was climbing steadily. Drake rarely brought the car to speeds over a hundred miles per hour, but he knew more than he'd ever known anything before that he wasn't moving fast enough. He let his lead foot press the pedal closer and closer to the floor mat.

He could see the BUD/S compound in his rearview mirror now, getting smaller and smaller with every second. That was the best view he'd ever had of it and probably the last he'd ever have of it.

A moment later, he heard a siren start up on the side of the road: speed trap. There was always a speed trap there. Drake had spotted it every time on the way to and from Imperial Beach. IB had the closest McDonald's to the base, except for those actually on the base, which often closed earlier than Drake's strawberry milkshake cravings hit him. IB was also the home of A.B. Brite Cleaners and Laundries. These days, everybody at BUD/S (including the instructor staff, unfortunately) knew that A.B. Brite was the place in town to take a uniform to get it professionally prepped for a BUD/S inspection or review board without actually having to put in the effort oneself.

Drake recognized the black cop car as being a 2007 Mustang GT, as were the majority of those he had seen patrolling the Coronado Island area. It was a nice car for a cop car, but wouldn't have been able to beat him to the border with a half-mile head start.

As Drake shifted his view back towards the road before him, he caught a glimpse of the seabag still sitting in the passenger seat, still loaded with the half-million dollars he had intended to pay Hodges as a fee for selling out

Stokley to him. Without having had Hodges assistance, it would have been considerably less likely that he'd ever have been able to discover Stokley's exact whereabouts in the first place.

Drake had signed his enlistment contract only six days after Hodges notified him of Stokley's return, just enough time for him to drive into town to verify that Stokley was, in fact, Stokley.

'Sorry Hodges, but it looks like I'm not going have a chance to get this to you after all. You'll just have to come down and pick it up yourself after things have cooled down.' Drake pulled the audio recorder out of his trouser pocket with his free hand and slipped it into the seabag. It would be more convenient to consolidate all of the incriminating evidence in case he needed to lose it on short notice.

After having spent the last week in Senior Chief Grand's office, the recorder would hopefully have accumulated implication of enough wrongdoing on the parts of Grand and Stokley to ensure that neither would be missed. It wasn't Drake's intention for their deaths to be ruled the unfortunate outcome of a random act.

Drake was becoming nauseous from the excitement. He feared it might cause him to vomit over himself, or worse, the pristine interior of the car, and opened both windows. It took him a second to adjust to the motion of the wind ripping violently through the car.

The Elephant Cages of the Naval Radio Station were coming up ahead on the right, which meant Drake was almost to IB. From there, it wouldn't be more than five miles to the border. Drake had driven the route several times before, just in case he'd ever have to use it. This would be the first time he actually crossed all the way over into Mexico, though. BUD/S trainees were strictly prohibited from crossing the border during their stay in Coronado. The word was that somebody in one of the classes before them, 'that guy,' had had a bit too much fun down there, and ruined the opportunity for everyone else.

A strange buzzing noise started up in the car all of a sudden, and then stopped. Drake glanced at the gauges behind the steering wheel, expecting to see a check engine light. It wasn't lit. The noise came back. Drake glanced down into the cup-holder at his side and saw his cell phone lighting up and vibrating among several loose quarters.

He looked at it, puzzled, for a moment before bringing it to his ear and answering, "Hello?"

"Seaman Drake, this is Chief Avilez. The quarterdeck watch just called me and we know what you've done. You're never going to get away from this. There's no place you can go where we won't find you. If you stop, I promise you won't be harmed until you've had a fair trial."

Drake was approaching IB. He took his foot off the gas for a moment to allow the vehicle to slow to a slightly more manageable speed as he began his pass through the small town. He could see the light at the intersection thirty yards ahead still red, but he didn't dare stop completely.

"I suppose it would be the same trial my father had. You had better -" Drake's speech paused as he passed through the midpoint of the intersection.

He swiveled his head barely in time to see an exceptionally broad set of longhorns mounted on the front of the brand new F-350 belonging, apparently, to '00BILLY' ram into the passenger side of the Porsche. He had just enough time before the impact to read the customized frame encasing the Texas license plate: 'Daddy bought it, but I got it!'

The Porsche was vaulted into the air. It was spinning uncontrollably, somewhat in the direction the truck had pushed it, still moving forward at nearly a hundred miles per hour.

"Hello? Drake?" The line had gone dead. Avilez hung up and threw his own cell phone onto the dashboard of the duty pick-up he was now driving at gratuitous speeds south towards Imperial Beach.

Drake was upside down, trying to regain some sort of directional bearing. The car had stopped moving. He had to wipe the blood running into his eyes from an unknown wound before he was able to see anything.

There was sound - music - coming from the radio. It must have been bumped on during the collision. Drake recognized the lyrics as Spanish but couldn't make out any of the words.

He looked out the window of the mangled, misshapen door on his side of the car. He saw the sign for a gas station and the pump standing adjacent to the Porsche, but couldn't find any other cars around him. The smell of gasoline was filling his nostrils. It was strong.

His vision was blurring. He reached with one hand to wipe his eyes out again, but unproductively. He was beginning to lose consciousness.

Drake scrambled through his daze to get out of the seatbelt. He fumbled with it a few times before it finally unlatched, and he fell into the roof of the car, but not in time to get out before his vision went completely black and he fainted.

Avilez was approaching IB. He could see the wreck up ahead. Drake's car was overturned at the foot of a leaking gas pump twenty yards from the intersection where it had been hit, and badly damaged. He slowed considerably as he passed through the intersection, the light green now, and pulled up to the parking lot of the gas station without entering it.

He put the car into park and jumped out. "Drake!" he yelled as he walked, pistol in hand, in the direction of the overturned Porsche. "Drake!" There was no human response coming from within, just the gentle playing of Latino music.

Avilez pointed the barrel of the weapon towards the car. He couldn't see Drake inside. His vision into the driver seat was blocked by the rear of the car as the driver's side faced away and towards the gas pump still dumping fuel all over the pavement. He started to yell out again, but the vehicle erupted into flames, igniting an instant later the pump next to which it had stopped.

Avilez was close enough to feel the heat of the blast on his skin, but still far enough not to be thrown by it. He reflexively brought both arms to his face to shield his burning eyes.

After a moment, he lowered them. His eyes were full of tears, but he could still see relatively clearly. The car was disintegrating before him. By the time anybody got here, there wouldn't be anything salvageable left of the car or its contents.

Avilez could hear sirens in the distance. He was

probably going to have to apologize to that officer in the Mustang for running him off the road a few miles back. He wouldn't be hurt, just really pissed off.

Avilez started to walk back towards his own vehicle, when something on the ground outside the entrance to the gas station caught his attention. It looked like a sea-bag. He walked over to it and nudged it with his boot to examine it from all sides.

The seabag appeared to be mostly empty, only a few chunky shapes huddled together near the bottom. The seabag wasn't locked but it was still latched shut. There was no name stenciled on it. Apart from a few scrapes, it wasn't noticeably damaged.

Avilez searched the main building of the gas station for surveillance cameras but found none. There weren't any bystanders nearby either. He picked up the bag and carried it back to the truck with him. It couldn't have weighed more than fifteen pounds. He dropped it onto the floor without looking inside.

The first of several police and emergency service vehicles was pulling up near his borrowed truck. Avilez saw the largest man he'd ever seen in any uniform waddling towards him at a startlingly slow speed. Avilez climbed into his truck and shut and locked the door, but rolled down the window.

"Afternoon, Sir," said the policeman in as calm a tone as he could manage.

"Afternoon," replied Avilez without getting out of the truck.

"You see what happened here?" The officer appeared to be breathing heavily. Avilez imagined that a man of his size must get winded simply by being. His massive gut caused his nametag to tilt upwards towards

Avilez. It read: Bigg. Avilez was convinced that the second 'g' must have been a typo.

"I drove in and saw that Porsche overturned by the gas station. It all went up in flames a moment later."

"Sir, I'm going to need to take down your information so that we'll be able to contact you at a later date if we need you to make a statement." The two exchanged information, Avilez making sure to get the man's full name, the Bigg of which was spelled with two 'g's, phone number, and identification number.

"Thank you, Mr. Avilez. We should be able to handle things from here." The man turned with a great deal of effort and began the trek back to his vehicle, a black Mustang GT.

17

Avilez started the ignition and began pulling back onto the road, facing north this time. He was careful to keep an eye out for approaching vehicles.

After a few yards, he was back to the intersection. The light was red and he stopped. He looked down at the seabag lying on the floor of the truck, in front of the passenger seat. 'What's in it?'

The light turned green. At the last second, Avilez put out his left turn signal and swerved south into Imperial Beach instead of following the highway back to the Naval Amphibious Base. He took the last right onto Palm Avenue heading west through IB towards the coast.

The pedestrians out on the town today were many, as usual. They came in all sorts, from tourists to legal residents of South California to illegal residents of South California, though it was sometimes hard to tell the latter two varieties apart. Most dressed in some combination of flip-flops, tank-tops, and bathing suits. Many were walking dogs or elderly relatives.

The avenue itself, like most of the streets in Imperial

Beach, was lined with palm trees and small restaurants. Avilez had been out to eat at some of them in the past.

After a couple hundred yards, Avilez approached El Tapatio Mexican Restaurant. He waited for a few seconds while a group of young Hispanic children crossed the crosswalk in front of the road named Silver Strand Boulevard (a back road which led through the Naval Radio Station before connecting with the highway Silver Strand Boulevard) before rounding the corner of El Tapatio and turning onto it himself. He'd be sure to stop by the small restaurant for some tacos to go on the way back.

Another two hundred and fifty yards down Silver Strand Boulevard and he was nearing the security check-point at the entrance to the United States Naval Radio Station. There was a single guard shack manned by a single guard, wearing the same rent-a-cop style uniform as those manning the gates outside the BUD/S compound and the NAB.

"Afternoon, Sir," was all the guard said to Avilez as he waived him through without checking ID. Apparently the presence of the duty vehicle and uniform was identification enough. Avilez said nothing in return, just smiled out the open window from behind his sunglasses.

Straight ahead down the gravel and dirt road before him were the Elephant Cages. Well over a hundred feet tall and roughly eight hundred feet in diameter, the forty-year-old submarine transmission interceptor encircled the lot containing Building 001.

From a distance, it looked as if it might have been intended to cage some enormous creature, but once one came within a few hundred feet, it was clear that the formation of wires and antennas was spread too openly to have fenced anything in or out.

Avilez ignored the sight for now and instead took a right turn onto the poorly maintained road that led back to the Seabee compound and Navy Leapfrog Parachute Team training building. He followed it for only a little ways before pulling off into the grass and parking, making sure not to hit any of the animal wildlife in the process, which included two gray-colored birds resembling cranes and several rodents too small to be squirrels but too big to be chipmunks.

He unbuckled his seatbelt and reached down under the passenger seat to retrieve the seabag. He toyed with it in his hands for a moment, trying to guess what it might contain from the way the contents shifted around inside, like a child would with a Christmas gift.

Eventually, his curiosity became too much and he had to open it. After surveying his surroundings briefly to make sure nobody else was around to watch him, he unlatched the top and peered inside.

"Sir, they both got here a couple hours ago," said Dr. Phay to the Executive Officer, standing beside him in the foyer of the BUD/S medical clinic. "We're really very lucky to have a medical clinic so close to the location of the incident."

"Are they both going to be alright?"

"The trainee, Dwayne, will be. The knife entered through the back of his neck and missed the majority of the critical items completely. It just grazed his jugular vein. I expect to be able to release him back to training in no more than one week, assuming his other injuries don't pose any significant setbacks in his recovery."

"What about Senior Chief Grand?"

"Grand, on the other hand, is in much worse condition. He has several wounds in the abdominal region and one across his neck. I'm surprised he's still alive. It's likely that he'll recover in time if we can keep him here and stable under close watch for the next couple weeks."

"Is the Senior Chief conscious?" asked Avilez, having just walked into the clinic.

"He wasn't the last I checked, but you're welcome to stop in and see him anyway. His is the first door on the right, down the hallway behind you."

"Chief, why don't you go check on Grand? I'm going to see how the trainee is doing."

"Yes, Sir," said Avilez to the XO, and they departed down different hallways.

Avilez reached the first set of doors and extended his hand doubtfully towards the knob of the door on the right. It was locked. He turned around and opened the door on the left. He walked in to examine the figure resting on the bed.

"Grand, wake up," he said after identifying it as being the Senior Chief. Grand groaned as he slowly opened his eyes. Avilez could see faintly that, under the thin white bed sheet, Grand was still wearing his boots and BDU trousers.

"Avilez, is that you? What's going on? Have you caught the trainee who did this yet?" Grand's voice sounded uneasy and concerned.

"That trainee is dead. He was incinerated in a car collision just outside of IB while I was in pursuit."

"That's good news." Grand sounded almost relieved, as much as any man potentially on his deathbed could.

"I suppose so, but what's not good news is the seabag

that was thrown from his car before it went up in flames." Avilez pulled the tape recorder he'd found inside the seabag out of his pocket and pressed the play button.

"His incompetence has already killed one innocent man, and effectively ruined your career as a SEAL in the process. He was a waste of life and now we've dealt with him. I'm about ready to move on and leave all this behind us," came Grand's rumbling, unmistakable voice. Avilez fast-forwarded the tape a few seconds and played it again. "I'll handle the money and make sure it ends up where it needs to be. Why don't you go get yourself some sleep, Hodges?" "Aye, aye, Senior Chief." Instead of pushing the stop button on the device, he pushed the record button.

"Which man are you talking about on the tape, Grand? Which guy did Stokley off?"

"I wouldn't say he 'offed' him. He killed him by accident in a car wreck while driving drunk a couple years ago. It was an English immigrant by the name of Derek Drake. Hodges was in the vehicle with him and nearly died too. That's where Stokley got that scar down his cheek, and where Hodges had the concussion that's kept him out of real action until now. I was the CDO at the time and helped them cover it up. Hodges and I decided everyone, including Stokley, would be better off if we just put him down for good. The man's had one chance after another to fix himself."

Grand started shifting in the bed. It looked as if he was trying to sit up. Avilez ran up to him and held him down as he spoke, "You're not going anywhere. I've got the money outside in the truck right now and I'm going to make sure it gets returned and that you get what you deserve for what you've done."

209

At first, Grand didn't speak. A second later, Avilez heard the safety click off of the handgun now pointed at his chest from underneath the hospital bed sheet. He slowly took his hands off Grand and backed away from him, unable to see exactly where the weapon was positioned.

Grand lifted the pistol, still trained on Avilez, out from under the covers. "I know what you think, Avilez. You think I'm a horrible man. You think I never deserved to wear this Trident in the first place. I haven't forgotten the oath I took to this country or to the Teams."

Avilez remained silent, keeping one eye on the pistol pointed at him, the other on the doorway eight yards away. It was too far to run. Grand was injured, but he wasn't dead yet.

"There is still nothing I wouldn't give to serve this country or the American people, nothing I wouldn't sacrifice to protect their way of life. I still am that man, Avilez." Grand brought the muzzle of the pistol to his own head and pulled the trigger.

Parts of his skull and brain were thrown into the wall next to him. Avilez remained were he stood. His finger pressed the stop button of the recorder in his hand.

"What just happened? What's going on in here?" The XO, HM1 Williams, and HM1 Boyle all rushed in at once. All had their own weapons drawn already.

"He's dead. He shot himself. I think you'll find everything you need on this tape. I'll be outside if you need anything." Avilez handed the recorder to the XO, who took it in one hand and examined it for a moment as he lowered his pistol back into the holster. When he looked up again, Avilez was already out the door and walking onto the grinder.

"We'll catch up with him later. Put your guns down and start getting this place cleaned up. No word of what you've seen here is to leave this room without my prior consultation. Am I understood?"

"Yes, Sir," they both answered. The XO departed briskly, tape in hand, back towards his office. He figured he'd listen to the tape before making an official decision on whether or not the incident here was worth interrupting the Commanding Officer's vacation.

18

02FEB1996: Recruit Training Command, Great Lakes, IL.

"Hey, little brother, congratulations! The guys and I were worried you weren't going to make it without us around to carry you."

"It looks like I managed."

"So, what they been teachin' you in this place? You get to shoot anyone yet?"

"No, it's mostly just been marching and shining shoes."

"Yeah, I can tell. You almost look like a real Sailor all dolled up in those whites."

"I guess so. It kind of feels good to put something nice on for once."

"Don't get too excited. You know they really don't give a shit about you, don't you?"

"What are you talking about?"

"As far as the Navy and all your so-called shipmates are concerned, you're just another dumb spic. To them, you're not any different than those fucking Puerto Rican putos who shot mom and dad."

"You're wrong. Nobody here cares what color I am or where I came from or which asshole older brother I had to put up with for eighteen years so why don't you just fuck off?"

"You need to get your head straight, Juanito. We're your family, always have been. Me and your brother, Jose, and the rest of the guys who watched your back all those years so you could dick around with your nose in a textbook and hold hands with your little chavalona, but you're a man now and it's time to start acting like it. It's time to start doing your part to make the name Avilez mean something."

"So what do you want me to do? I'm signed on for six years. I couldn't leave even if I wanted to."

"You don't have to. Stay in training. Go play Navy SEAL for a while. And when you come home, you can teach us some of that commando shit so we can finally get rid of all the Rafters and Cacos movin' into our turf."

"I'm not going back. This is home now."

By now, his relief would have taken over the watch for him, so Avilez headed instead for the beach.

He walked over the berm and down to the waterline. He stayed just out of reach of the tide to keep the shine on his shoes from getting damaged. It had been awfully tempting for him to just make off with the money himself. There must have been close to half a million dollars in that seabag. There was also still the question of how to handle Hodges, but that would be somebody else's problem now. Avilez had done his part. His train of thought returned to the money. It was still sitting out in the duty truck where he'd left it.

He hiked back over the berm and past the CBH to the grinder outside the first phase office, but the truck wasn't there. Avilez ran across the grinder and into the wreckage of the quarterdeck.

"Where's the white F-250 that was parked out on the grinder earlier this morning?" he asked one of the trainees still on watch.

"Chief, about five minutes after you returned it, Instructor Hodges checked it out. He said he might need it for a while."

"Did he give any hints of where he might be going?"

"Negative, Chief. He just took off heading south on the strand."

Avilez could feel his heart sinking. That would have been almost an hour ago. By now, Hodges would have long since crossed the border into Mexico, with the five hundred thousand, and could be on a plane to any place in the world by tonight.

He decided to go through the motions of trying to stop him anyway. He pulled his cell phone out of his trouser pocket and dialed the XO's number.

"Hello?"

"Sir, this is Chief Avilez. I think Hodges may have gotten away."

"We figured as much. I'm at the combat training tank with 269 as we speak. Peterson and Dunn said Hodges left over an hour ago without saying where he was going or when he'd be back."

"Sir, I have reason to believe he's taken one of the duty vehicles across the border and that he has the money Senior Chief Grand procured for Drake, possibly from the BUD/S emergency fund."

"Well, if he's already in Mexico, there's not a whole lot we can do now. I'm assuming the truck will turn up sooner rather than later, but he won't be with it. I think it would be best if you went home and took the rest of the day off, Chief."

"I'll do that, Sir. Give me a call if anything comes up." Avilez hung up the phone.

What to do now, he thought. He supposed he could just go back home and cry himself to sleep over the whole thing like the XO had ordered. 'No,' he decided, 'best to give that cop a call before they start calling me.' Seaman Apprentice Drake had no known living relatives and somebody was going to have to officially identify the remains as being his, even if by no other means than evaluating the fact that they were what remained of the man driving Seaman Apprentice Drake's Porsche. Avilez was Drake's class proctor, the CDO on duty at the time, and the last one to talk to Drake. He'd be they one they'd call.

Avilez picked up his phone and dialed the number he'd been provided by Officer Bigg. He reached a receptionist with an unusually sexy phone voice. He wondered if she was wearing any underwear.

"Officer Bigg, please."

"Yes, Sir. Hold on one moment, please." He endured a few seconds of classical music.

"Officer Bigg."

"Hello, Officer. This is Chief Petty Officer Juan Avilez with the United States Navy. We spoke earlier today."

"Oh, hello, Sir. What's on your mind?"

"I just wanted to call and see if you needed to schedule me to come in and identify the remains of Seaman Apprentice Sidney Drake, the man driving the gray Porsche at the time of the collision earlier this morning."

"No, that won't be necessary at all. Even if you could bring us his dental records or some other description of him, there aren't ever enough remains left to identify the victim of an incident like this one. There's probably nothing more than a pile of ash left of him now."

215

'Of course there isn't.'

"Okay, Sir, let me know if you need anything else." Avilez hung up the phone. Now it was time to go home and cry himself into an early afternoon slumber.

19

17MAR2008: Inside the Galley of the Naval Amphibious Base, Coronado, CA.

"Good morning, team. I hope everyone enjoyed their weekend off and is ready to start back up. We meet our next class for the first time this morning," said Avilez as he approached the galley table manned by Instructors Peterson, Dunn, and Manson who was new to the first-phase staff, as well as HM1 Boyle.

"We're ready. I don't know if *they* are," said Instructor Dunn as he pointed to the fresh crop of about a hundred and seventy trainees seated thirty yards away at the far end of the galley. In their sparkling new BDUs and unscathed boots, they looked immaculately clean and neat, not to mention healthy, like the perfectly manicured lawn everybody's dog is so determined to plant a turd on. By the end of the day, the instructor staff would have planted that turd.

"They just got here from Great Lakes. They had their gear issue last week, so we officially kick off their indoctrination in twenty minutes."

217

"Hey, check out what's on the news. They've been replaying the same footage since I woke up this morning," said Boyle.

Avilez turned his chair around to get a better view of the television mounted high on the wall behind him. He stared at the mug shot gazing indifferently out from the upper right hand corner of the screen for several seconds before the words of the reporter began to register with him.

"...the man, who has since been identified as former Navy SEAL Taylor Hodges, was contracting through the private military corporation TCC International under the alias Michael Wooldridge. His is the first contractor death reported in the region since last summer, though it will be the 241st American civilian contractor death since March of 2003. The circumstances surrounding the incident are still unclear..."

"So that's where he ran off to. I wonder what happened to the money," said Dunn.

"Who cares? Anyone who would have wanted to use it is dead now," said Peterson.

"What are you talking about? I would've loved the chance to give half of it to my ex-wife."

"Anyway, I guess Taylor finally got what he'd been thirsting for. After going through BUD/S for over two years, he was finally given the chance to go down range and die for his country."

"Let's not over-glorify him. The man's still a murderer and a thief. Maybe DEVGRU hunted him down and offed him. They could have made it look like some rag-head did it," suggested SO1 Manson. It was clear that the others sitting at the table disapproved of Manson's disregard for what remained of Hodges' dignity, but nobody could say he was wrong.

Avilez didn't know who had killed Taylor Hodges, whether it be another SEAL platoon; a still vengeful young man who may or may not have survived a horrific car collision six weeks prior and may or may not have held a grudge against Hodges for failing to bring Stokley to justice when he had the chance three years ago; or an actual Iraqi militant; but Avilez didn't really care. The infection that had manifested itself at BUD/S was now gone, and the program was once again in a position to continue on as it had for decades, selecting and training future Navy SEALs.

The soon-to-be Senior Chief dug his fork into the burnt galley omelet resting ominously in the center of an otherwise empty plate. He brought a bite to his face and sniffed it. It smelled bad. He put it in his mouth and starting chewing. It tasted bad, too.

Acknowledgements

This novel is a work of fiction. The undeniable actuality of some of the facts within is a result of my attempt, as the author, to produce and enhance the factual weight and feeling of authenticity of the story. Those specific details included in the description of items such as the Elephant Cages and IBS boats are based entirely on information obtainable from resources belonging to the public domain and are, to the best of my knowledge, accurate and precise.

However, the plot, characters, and events existing or taking place within the story are solely products of my own imagination and are in no form built upon the existence or occurrence of actual people or events. It is not my intention to replicate within this novel the experiences of any BUD/S class (including class 269), any current or former BUD/S instructor, or any current or former BUD/S trainee.

There has also been some very minor application of the artistic license, most notably in the mention of BUD/S class 269's pass through the Naval Special

Warfare Preparatory Course (BUD/S Prep). The first class for which such a preparatory course was implemented was BUD/S class 270. Additionally, certain chronological checkpoints on the timelines of BUD/S class 269 and SWCC class 59-2 have been approximated and deviate slightly from the actual times at which they occurred.

I owe thanks to those who suffered through unfinished drafts of this work during its production and provided insights on the presentation of the content and progression of the story.

Glossary

269: 'Winter' BUD/S class beginning first phase in early 2008.

Bates 922: Eight-inch leather boot worn by Naval personnel, especially BUD/S and SWCC trainees.

BCT: Basic Crewman Training – SWCC pipeline training phase similar in purpose and content to BUD/S.

BDU: Battle Dress Uniform – United States military's standard uniform for combat situations and simulations since 1981, now being phased out and replaced.

BIC: Shaving the head smooth with a 'BIC' razor, or similar disposable razor.

blue-and-gold: BUD/S or SWCC instructor; term derived from the navy blue T-shirts with gold lettering 'UDT/SEAL Instructor' or 'SWCC Instructor' worn by said instructors.

boat-crew: Unit of seven BUD/S trainees; organized by height; the smallest boat-crew and tallest boat-crew are sometimes referred to as the Smurfs and Jolly Greens respectively.

BSRB: Brown-Shirt Rollback – a post-Hellweek BUD/S trainee, or 'Brown-Shirt,' who has been rolled back in training.

BUD/S: Basic Underwater Demolition/SEAL – six month training period in the SEAL training pipeline preceding jump school and SQT; broken into three phases following a three-week orientation/indoctrination.

CBH: Combined Bachelor Housing – barracks housing Sailors of any rank.

CMC: Command Master Chief – Master Chief Petty Officer highest in the chain of command of a naval command.

CO: Commanding Officer – commissioned officer highest in

the chain of command a naval command.

CQT: Crewman Qualification Training – similar in purpose to SQT, but attended instead by SWCC candidates; one CQT class consists of two BCT classes, for instance, BCT classes 59-1 and 59-2 combine to form CQT class 59.

crow: Petty Officer - enlisted Sailor occupying the pay-grades of E-4 to E-6; can also refer to the rank insignia of enlisted Sailors in pay-grades E-4 to E-6.

deck: Navy and Marine term meaning 'floor;' can mean the floor in general, a floor of a building, etc.

DOR: Drop on Request – voluntary removal from training.

drying cages: Chain-link building outside the first phase BUD/S and SWCC barracks lined with several rows of cubbies; used to house and air-dry swimming gear and life-vests between water evolutions and IBS evolutions.

EMI: Extra Military Instruction – Additional duty generally assigned to personnel as remediation.

ERV: Emergency Rescue Vehicle – Vehicle adapted to fit the role of an ambulance or transport and distribute basic first aid supplies.

galley: Navy term for cafeteria, dining facility, chow hall, etc.

grinder: Paved lot, especially the BUD/S parking lot outside the first phase office.

head: Navy and Marine term for restroom.

Hellweek: One hundred and thirty-two hour period beginning the Sunday after week three of first phase during which trainees will be put through a series of back-to-back physical evolutions without receiving more than four hours total of sleep, but being fed exactly every six hours.

Hoo-yah: Term utilized by Sailors, especially BUD/S trainees, to express a variety of emotions, acknowledge an order, or signal affirmation of a statement or question.

IBS: Inflatable Boat-Small - small, soft-hull, inflatable rubber boat used by first phase BUD/S trainees for several training evolutions including surf passage, land portage, and rock portage.

ITB: Iliotibial Band − longitudinal, fibrous reinforcement of the deep tissues of the thigh extending from the gluteus maximus downward to the outside of the knee.

leaning rest: 'Up' push-up position; the back should be straight and the head up.

LPO: Leading Petty Officer − position held by the most senior member of a naval division in the pay-grades of E-4 to E-6.

MRE: Meal Ready to Eat − portable, pre-packaged, freeze-dried meal edible with little or no preparation

"Navy SEALs:" 1990 movie directed by Lewis Teague starring Charlie Sheen and Michael Biehn

NCO: Non-commissioned Officer − enlistee occupying the pay-grades of E-4 to E-9; Petty Officers and Chief Petty Officers in the Navy; Corporals and Sergeants in other branches.

NEX: Navy Exchange − general store for Sailors stocking food, uniform items, and daily necessities.

OIC: Officer in Charge − officer in charge of a naval division or detachment, usually a commissioned officer.

POV: Privately Owned Vehicle − civilian vehicle owned and operated by military personnel.

PT: Physical Training − physical exercise and conditioning, existing in a variety of forms.

rack: Navy and Marine term for bunk, or bed.

rate: Term indicating the rank and specialty of Navy enlisted personnel; for example: HMSN – Hospital Corpsman Seaman (Hospitalman), AO1 – Aviation Ordnanceman First Class Petty Officer, SOCS: Special Warfare Operator Senior Chief Petty Officer.

Seabag: Durable, green, Navy and Marine issue duffel bag.

SEAL: Sea Air Land – variety of U.S. Naval Special Forces troop characterized by adaptability and diversity in deployment theaters.

SO: Special Warfare Operator – official Navy rating classification for SEALs.

SOCOM: (United States) Special Operations Command.

SQT: SEAL Qualification Training – five month training period immediately preceding the SEAL trainees' pinning ceremony.

SWCC: Special Warfare Combatant-craft Crewman – variety of Naval Special Forces troop specializing in small combatant-craft operation in combat zones; represented by the rating classification 'SB' meaning 'Small Boat.'

Trident Pin: Gold warfare device worn on the uniforms of Navy SEALs; consists of an eagle, a trident, an anchor, and a flintlock pistol.

UDT: Underwater Demolition Team(s) – Navy Special Forces sector active from 1942 until 1983; precursor to the Navy SEALs; specialized in pre-amphibious landing hydrographic reconnaissance as well as water-based demolition.

XO: Executive Officer – officer second in command to the Commanding Officer.

About the Author

Zeph Stone is a United States Navy
Sailor who is currently serving on
active duty. His enlistment has
included several months of training
in the Special Warfare Community.